THE
FOOTBALL WARS

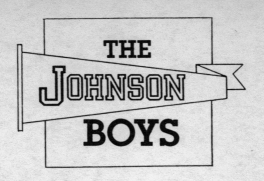

THE
FOOTBALL WARS
SCOTT ELLER

AN
APPLE
PAPERBACK

SCHOLASTIC INC.
New York Toronto London Auckland Sydney

ISBN 0-590-42828-4

12 11 10 9 8 7 6 5 4 3   2 3 4 5 6 7/9

Printed in the U.S.A.   28

First Scholastic printing, September 1992

THE
FOOTBALL WARS

1.
Pik

Pik was mad. He was woozy, and mad. His nose was bleeding. He unsnapped his chinstrap and tilted his helmet back on his head to check the damage. Both nostrils were bleeding, and the bridge of his nose was cut, too. He looked over at Ronnie Duggan, who was looking back at him with satisfaction from where the offense was huddling. Ronnie pointed to his own nose beneath the face mask and smiled.

Ronnie had head-butted him on his last rush. During the count Pik had only been half-concentrating; at the snap he'd come up hard out of his stance and Ronnie, instead of backpedalling into his pass-blocking stance, had driven forward, helmet down, into Pik's face. Pik had been flattened onto his back, a pancake, the worst thing that could happen in practice besides an injury. Ronnie had taken his time getting up, and Pik had finally thrown him off.

Pik closed his eyes, standing there on the line

of scrimmage, and shook his head to clear it. The blood helped him focus. It tasted salty, and gritty with dirt.

"Hey, Pik," Gabriel said, behind him. Gabriel was the strong safety. He kept an eye out for anyone who might've had their bell rung. "Pik."

Pik strapped on his helmet and turned around. He grinned, hoping he looked grisly and frightening, a psycho capable of anything.

"Very nice," Gabriel said. He did, actually, look a little envious, though no amount of war paint was worth the humiliation of getting pancaked. "Earth calling, Pik. We home?"

"I'm home," Pik said. "And now I'm going to go visiting in Mr. Duggan's neighborhood." He turned away from Gabriel. The offense was coming out to the line of scrimmage, Ronnie Duggan in front of Pik, setting his legs and digging in. Pik slipped his mouthpiece back in and got down in his stance, digging his left cleat and hand in up front and kicking his right leg back for maximum off-the-ball power. He was a rocket, a missile, a laser. Ronnie was not in trouble, Ronnie was history; Ronnie was old news, Ronnie was dead. Ronnie was Wile E. Coyote, with his ears drooped and his eyes huge, and Pik was the anvil dropped from two miles up.

"He all right?" he heard Ray DeVellis say from back in his position at middle linebacker. He never

2

says more than two words, Pik thought. That was three.

"I think we're gonna be asking that about Ronnie in around six seconds," he heard Andy, at free safety, answer.

Tony Picarazzi, a stubby kid, short for quarterback, who always wore shoe polish under his eyes to cut down glare (he said), was over the center and calling signals. He had an eye out for Pik.

Roll away from me, Pik thought, twitching and flinching in anticipation. Roll all the way to China. I'll hunt you down.

At the snap, Tony was up and backpedalling but that wasn't what had Pik's immediate attention. Pik exploded up and out of his stance with a first step that Ronnie Duggan couldn't handle in his dreams on his best day and, instead of using that speed to just blow around Ronnie, he drove his shoulder into Ronnie's sternum, lifting both of the kid's feet off the ground. In the space of time it took Ronnie to come back down, Pik had driven by him with Tony Picarazzi as his new goal. He felt Ronnie's arms trying to trip him as he went by, and noticed the halfback trying to cut his legs, but nothing distracted him from goal number one: putting Tony Picarazzi on his back before he could get rid of the ball. Tony scrambled right, running with the impressive speed that fear can generate.

3

In his peripheral vision Pik could see Ray sliding along the line of scrimmage to shut Tony off to the sidelines. He knew that at some point Tony was going to have to pull up or cut upfield, and he realized that he looked forward to that moment.

The moment came; Tony planted his feet and hoped against hope to squeeze around the corner, all notion of throwing the ball gone now. When Tony cut, Pik went airborne, arms out and legs up, Batman swooping from roof to roof, a black figure that blots out the sun. He caught Tony flush in the back and the two of them flew out of bounds with such force that they flattened two bench-warmers, an equipment manager, and a practicing cheerleader who'd just stopped to tie her shoes.

"My head," Tony said from underneath him, when they finally stopped bouncing. "My head. Have you seen it?"

"Guy's crazy," one of the benchwarmers said, picking himself off the ground.

Their coach was standing over them. He said, "Telander, your intensity seems to be coming and going today."

"Mostly coming and going over me," Tony said. He was smeared with white chalk from the side-line markers. He looked at his hand, flexing it to see if it still moved.

Pik freed an arm and spit his mouthpiece out.

4

It swung around off the bottom of his face mask. "I'm saving something for the game, Coach," he said. As he sat there tangled with Tony, the blood from his nose mixed with his sweat and got in his eyes; he squinted to clear them.

"How about saving our second string quarterback for the game, as well?" Coach said. "If you go ahead and kill Tony here, what'll we do if Fixx gets hurt?"

"Thanks, Coach," Tony said.

"No problem," Coach said.

Gabriel and Andy were standing over Pik, helping him up. "That was a major-league rush," Gabriel said. "I'm not sure Anthony Muñoz woulda handled that one."

"I'd like to find out," Tony said. Andy was standing him on his feet.

"Great discussion we're having, kiddies," Coach said. "But this is practice. You know, where we run through various plays so that we don't embarrass ourselves when we play another team, like Milford? Tomorrow?"

"Right, Coach," Tony said, heading back to the offense's huddle. "Hey, Duggan," he called as he trotted over. "Next time yell, 'Look out!' "

Ronnie glared over at him and then at Pik.

On the next play, Pik took an inside move and Ronnie grabbed his face mask and twisted, wrenching him down to the ground. They shoved at each other in the pileup at the line of scrimmage. On the play after that, Ronnie tried to grab his throat and Pik gave him a head slap that rocked him back on his heels.

"Take it easy out there," Coach said, but he wasn't looking up. Pik wasn't even sure he meant them.

"C'mon. C'mon," Ronnie was yelling from under his lowered helmet. His face was screwed up as if he hated Pik and Pik's whole family. His mouthpiece was in, so what he was saying was comically garbled.

"I guh take you out," he said.

"Uh uh uh uh," Pik said. He made a face like Ronnie's to show him how stupid he looked.

Pik could hear that Tony was calling an audible; a sweep, he guessed, to Pik's side. The standard thing to control a problem rusher, and give the blocker a little confidence at the same time.

So Pik was ready. At the snap, Ronnie roared up at him, frustrated, yet shouting with intensity and ready to return some of the punishment. Pik met him with extended arms, shivering his momentum to a dead stop, controlling him by getting under his shoulder pads, and wrestling him laterally to keep him in front of the intended avenue for the sweep. He strung the play out that way, Ronnie's feet churning uselessly to drive him upfield, while Robin Lenz, their starting cornerback, took out the lead blocker. Gabriel and Andy swooped in to help with the run from their safety positions. Pik drove Ronnie so far back that the runner collided with him going the other way, tripping and stumbling, and then the pile was swarmed under by Gabriel and Andy.

Ronnie came out of the pile swinging. Pik avoided the swing, and stood up a little taller for everyone to see, as if saying, "What the heck's going on *here*?"

Some of the other offensive linemen got their arms around Ronnie, and dragged the two apart.

"Great defense," Coach called, as if absent-mindedly, from the sidelines. "Horrible offense. Everybody take five."

The defense streamed off the field, tired and happy to be dominant, even if a lot of the offense was second-string. A lot of them, including Gabriel, Andy, and Pik, played both ways, so that when the offense practiced, some second stringers filled in on defense and, when the defense practiced, scrubeenies had to stand in there, too. It was good practice for the scrubeenies, anyway, even if they usually took a beating. Gabriel, Andy, and Pik were first string on both squads, so their side usually dominated in practice.

They flopped down together at one end of the bench. The equipment manager's identification tape was still on the back of Andy's and Gabriel's helmets: Pik could read the *Kim* and *Fixx* hand-lettered in magic marker. He'd seen a picture once of the Minnesota Vikings practicing, tagged with the same little markers, so it didn't seem bush league to him.

"You and tubby were starting to get a little carried away out there, weren't you?" Gabriel asked.

"Here I am going at half-speed and he drills me. I couldn't believe it," Pik said.

Gabriel laughed. "You gonna do something about your face?" he asked. "You look like one of those *Friday the 13th* guys got you."

"I'm going to school like this," Pik replied.

"It'll cover some of the dirt," Andy said.

Pik shoved him, and Andy gave him a whap on the side of his helmet. They hunched forward, rubbing sore spots, and looking down the bench where Coach was going over his clipboard, preparing for the last drills of the day. Pik's ankle was sore, and he figured he'd twisted it somewhere in that last sequence of downs.

Today was the last day of football practice before the season opener against Milford at Milford, Friday night. It was their second season on the team and already they were pretty much the biggest stars: Pik at defensive end and wide receiver on offense, Gabriel at strong safety and quarterback, and Andy at free safety and halfback. Gabriel and Andy, who always got their homework in and did it right yet never seemed geeky, liked offense better. Of course, Pik, who spent most of his time being asked, "Why can't you be more like those nice boys Gabriel and Andy?" liked defense better.

Gabriel liked throwing touchdown passes: twenty-five yards on a line, corner of the end zone. Andy liked scoring on long runs: outrunning the defense even when it had the pursuit angle on him. Pik liked hitting people. Pik liked best what he'd just been doing: dominating one guy on the way to terrorizing another.

The last practice drills before a game were always for the special teams. For Pik and Gabriel and Andy that meant field goals, with Gabriel holding, Andy kicking, and Pik lined up as usual opposite Ronnie, trying to spike it back in their faces. Coach announced the drill and they got up together, strapping on the old Riddells as they headed out to the twenty-yard line. Andy practiced longer field goals alone.

"I'm gonna get one today," Pik said, as they split up: Andy and Gabriel over with the offense, Pik to the defense.

"Gimme a break," Andy said over his shoulder. "You'll be lucky to see it go over."

"Doleman," Pik called to him. Together the three of them had watched a Vikings-Bears game in which Chris Doleman, the Vikings' All-Pro defensive end, had blocked two field goals, including the potential game-winner.

Pik got down in his stance opposite Ronnie again. "How're things, Ronnie?" he said. "Having a good day?"

Ronnie growled.

Gabriel was calling the signals. At the snap everything went wrong for them: Pik had it anticipated perfectly (it helped knowing Gabriel so well), and Gabriel, catching him coming in the corner of his eye, bobbled the ball momentarily. Ronnie had expected the outside rush and was too late in recovering to prevent Pik from squeezing through inside. Pik got his hands clear and up, just over his head, and *bap!* hit the ball with both palms, ricocheting it back over their heads. Ronnie tackled him, but everyone else took off after the ball, and Gabriel ended up having to tackle Robin Lenz, who'd scooped the ball up on the way to the end zone.

Andy stood where his swing had left him, his head down and his hands on his hips. "*Darn* it," he said. Andy didn't swear. Another reason parents liked him.

"You're gonna wanna watch that language," Pik said, getting up.

"Shut up," Ronnie said.

"Who's talking to you?" Pik snapped.

"Shut up," Ronnie repeated.

"Oh, Duggan," Pik said, feeling the sting in his palms from the impact of the ball. "Sometimes I'm so glad I'm not you."

"Let's go, let's go here," Coach called. "Nice job, Telander. Offense: you're now down 7–0 if Gabriel doesn't make that tackle. Let's do it again."

They lined up and ran the play again. Ronnie got a good piece of Pik, who didn't get good penetration but got his arms up. Andy kicked it low, into the pile.

The defensive players stood around celebrating.

"Offense!" Coach called. "What's the deal? Do we think we can get a kick off here, or what? We've been practicing this for twenty minutes now and nothing's cleared the line of scrimmage."

Andy was upset, you could see. Gabriel was trying to calm him down. Normally, Pik would've been helping out, too, but they were on opposite sides, at least for now.

They lined up with fire in their eyes. At the snap, Pik got a trio of shocks: Ronnie rocked him with a hit; at the same time, someone else cut Pik's legs and, as he fell backward and the bodies collapsed on top of him from all angles, he heard the boom of Andy's foot meeting the ball, as loud a boom as he'd ever heard.

He didn't see the field goal. He heard the awed

sounds from those above him who did, though. And when he got up and looked off in the direction of the goal posts, he saw the equipment manager running off into the distance after the ball. The kid was twenty yards from the back of the end zone already and still going.

"How far did that thing *go*?" he asked someone who'd helped him up.

"Mars," the guy said. "Pluto."

Gabriel was hugging Andy with congratulations, as were other members of the kicking team. Coach said from the sidelines, "See what happens when we actually get a kick off, offense?" But even he sounded a little awed.

"Great kick, Kim," Pik called over to Andy. "I'm coming after the next one, though."

"Come on ahead," Andy called back. "The way I'm gonna kick it, you get your hand in front of it, it's your funeral."

Pik lined up again, raring to go until he remembered that *boom*, and then his hands opened and closed anxiously, as if worried about themselves.

They ran the play four or five more times, until Coach was satisfied. Andy kicked well, though he didn't get off any more cannon shots. Everything worked for the kicking team. Andy's kicks were straight. Gabriel's holds were clean. Everybody blocked. Ronnie did his job with Pik. There was a bang-bang quality to everything that pleased everyone, and made them feel like they were older.

And it was only afterward, on the way home, with Gabriel and Andy and Pik taking turns shoving each other into and over puddles, that Gabriel and Andy remembered to razz Pik for not getting his hands too far in the air, after he'd heard the boom of that first big kick.

2.
Gabriel

Something was wrong. Gabriel had the feeling he occasionally got in bad dreams, that something was wrong, that something important was different from the way it looked, and that he was the only one who noticed.

Here they'd been sailing along in their first game of the season, Milford at Milford, "kicking tail and taking names," as Coach Kohut liked to say. A beautiful Friday night: the stars out, and enough wind to keep you chilly and charged up. They'd come out from the opening kickoff and done everything right, executing on offense and defense. It was Johnson Junior High's first offensive play of the new season, and Gabriel's first official snap after having taken over from Tony Picarazzi, last year's starter. Gabriel rifled a twenty-two-yarder to Pik, nailing him right in the numbers. On the second play, Andy hit a quick opener for another seventeen. After a brisk six-play drive they'd gone ahead 7–0, with Gabriel scoring on a naked bootleg so easily that he'd held the ball up in celebration while still on the five-yard line.

Their defense had held, too, on its first set of downs, Pik playing, despite his bad ankle, with his usual manic abandon, and Milford's offense had done a three-and-out. Johnson scored on its second possession, and again on its third. At the end of the first quarter, with the score 21–0, Milford's quarterback had taken to rolling out and slinging it downfield as far as he could, a sure sign of a panicked offense. They'd regroup a little at the half, probably, but by then things would be out of hand.

On one of those run-for-cover rollouts, the quarterback cocked his arm and promptly had it stripped by Pik, who'd come all the way around from the other side on an outside rush. In the chaos as the ball got kicked around, Ray DeVellis picked it up on the dead run and scored with Milford's halfback still hanging on his shoulder, trying somehow to bring him down.

But that was when things changed. Johnson's kicking team lined up for the extra point. Gabriel called the signals and took the snap, concentrating on receiving the ball clean and spinning the laces away from Andy's oncoming foot. So he had no idea what hit him.

He was flattened, annihilated. Andy never got the kick off. When everyone unpiled, Andy helped

15

him up. Gabriel stood there a minute, woozy, thinking, *27–0, four touchdowns can beat us now*, and caught Ronnie Duggan's eyes, and froze: Ronnie was smiling.

Andy led him back to the bench, Gabriel more unsettled now by the smile than by the hit. He said, "Whose guy was that?" but he already knew the answer: Ronnie's.

Back on the bench he considered telling Andy, but thought he should wait. What was the point of bringing it up now? Ronnie had wanted his one shot at revenge, and he'd gotten it. Gabriel would settle with him later, privately.

He sat on the bench, thinking about it. Coach had decided to spell him for a series on defense, or until he remembered what country he was in, as Coach put it.

He wasn't used to people being mad at him. It unnerved him. He wanted to believe everyone liked him, all the time, and that whenever anyone didn't, it was because of a misunderstanding that could be cleared up.

But he knew this wasn't a misunderstanding. Ronnie didn't like him because: a) he was Pik's friend, and b) he'd taken over the quarterbacking job from Tony Picarazzi, who was Ronnie's friend. Tony was okay — Tony could live with it — but Ronnie and his pals on the offensive line took it harder than Tony had; and besides, they thought the SuperFriends, as they called Gabriel, Pik, and Andy, were way too stuck up.

At one point a week or so ago, Ronnie and the rest of the offensive line — Lenny Marcus, Dave Booth (who had the worst teeth of anybody Gabriel'd ever seen, real scuzzy things), Charlie Izzo, and this incredible no-neck geek named Lynn Freed — had come across Gabriel, Pik, and Andy having one of their own mini-practices, just hacking around, really. Booth had said, showing off his bad teeth, "Oh, look. Donatello, Michaelangelo, and Raphael." And Andy had replied, "That's truer than you know, pal. When it comes to this game, we're artists. You guys're brick-layers."

And it was true: They weren't a bad offensive line, as things went, but they weren't exactly the strength of the team, either. When they did their job they were good enough to open some cracks for Andy to squeeze through, or provide Gabriel with enough of a shaky pocket to allow him to improvise or hit his primary receiver.

Milford scored. Pik came back to the bench swearing.

"What happened?" Gabriel asked. Pik poured himself a cup of Gatorade from the thermos bucket and then threw the full cup on the field. Someone on the kickoff team kicked it back to the sidelines.

"Aaah, a little counter draw," Andy said, disgusted. "They suckered us."

Gabriel shook his head, feeling a little responsible — the counter draw was one of the strong safety's prime responsibilities — and, knowing that, he promised himself it would be the last time *that* worked for Milford.

Milford was a little fired up now that it was 27–7. Gabriel came out to the offensive huddle last, checking his field position. He leaned into the huddle to call the play. He caught Ronnie's eyes, and Marcus's, and then Booth's. He stumbled on the play call, a little shook up.

"You all right?" Andy asked him in a low voice as they came out of the huddle.

"Right as rain," Gabriel said. "Cowabunga."

He'd called a buttonhook to Pik, with Andy as a safety valve out in the flat if Pik drew double coverage. He looked over the defense and, satisfied with what he saw, decided against calling an audible.

At the snap, he backpedalled into position, saw Pik come clear, and then was wiped out.

How he hung onto the ball, he had no idea.

In the huddle Ronnie said, "My goof. Sorry. It won't happen again."

It looked like Booth was stifling a laugh.

"Brush your teeth, Booth," Gabriel said.

On second down and long he called a rollout. Ronnie, leading the blocking on that side, tripped, and Milford's defensive end found himself right where Gabriel wanted to be, and almost took Gabriel's head off.

"What's going on here?" Andy said. Gabriel was sitting on his rear, shaking it off. He felt nauseous from the hit.

Pik looked at the offensive line. "You guys having any trouble?" he said ominously. "Maybe some of you want to take a breather?"

"We're fine," Ronnie said. "Maybe *you* guys should take a break."

It was third-and-twenty-five. Andy took Gabriel's arm in the huddle and said, "Let me take it."

So Gabriel called Andy's number on a delayed draw. The offensive line blocked well. Andy got fourteen yards of it back, but Johnson had to punt.

Coach called a timeout before the change of possession. As they came off the field, he said, clapping his hands, "Little breakdown, little breakdown, but we'll get it back."

Ray DeVellis came over to where Gabriel was standing. "What's going on here?" Ray asked. Pik and Andy had come over, too. When *Ray* asked a question, you knew something was up.

"I'm not sure yet," Gabriel said, though he was. He stayed out for a play before he joined the rest of the defense. It felt like a relief to hit instead of getting hit. Milford got a first down or two and then had to punt when Andy and Gabriel sandwiched a receiver on a deep pattern and broke up the pass.

On Johnson's next offensive series Gabriel called a quick hitter to Pik: a slant pass that would allow him to get the ball off so quickly it wouldn't matter what the blocking was. The play went for eleven yards when Pik broke a tackle. Gabriel called the play again, and it worked again for seven. On second-and-three he called for a hitch-and-go, a deep pattern for all the marbles to Pik.

"Don't let me down, here," he said to the offensive line, peering at them in the huddle. "Give me the time."

They did. No one got near him. He had all day. Pik's inside hitch left his double coverage dazed and confused and he went straight down the sidelines, free and clear and beautiful. Gabriel hung the ball out there, a beautiful arc, a perfect spiral, a zeppelin of a catchable pass; and Pik ran under it at full throttle and skimmed into the end zone — Marino to Duper, Montana to Rice, something for the highlight clips, if only Johnson had highlight clips. Sixty-six yards and the score was now 33–7. The extra point made it 34.

Gabriel came off the field after the successful extra point, figuring he'd let the thing with Ronnie go, that maybe he'd been imagining some of it, and maybe it was all over.

Milford fumbled the next kickoff. There was a scramble and, in the confusion, somebody on Johnson came up with the ball in the end zone. Just like that it was 41–7, and it was still the first half.

It was pretty shocking, really, because Milford wasn't that bad.

While he was getting ready to go in on defense, Gabriel saw Ronnie talking to Coach. He knew immediately what Ronnie was saying: let Picarazzi in; the game's over, use the rest of the time to see what Picarazzi can do.

He was distracted by that during his defensive series, but it didn't matter because Milford's quarterback was now so rattled he threw two passes into the dirt and one into the stands. Pik came off the field cackling the way he did when he smelled the kill.

"Coach?" Gabriel called, as the offense ran out onto the field. He gestured to himself, as if to ask, Want me to go back in?

"You the quarterback, or not?" Coach called. "How hard were you hit that last time?"

So Gabriel ran out onto the field after the punt. When he got to the huddle it was clear that Ronnie and the rest of the line did not want him there.

They were on their own twenty-two, and there was only a minute or so left in the first half. "Let's just take it into the half the way it is," he said, apologetically. Then he caught himself and thought, What am I talking like *this* for? I'm apologizing to *them*?

"Sure, sure," Ronnie said, looking up at him from his lowered helmet.

They ran the ball, no frills, and everybody blocked. Milford didn't try to stop the clock.

In the locker room at halftime, Coach went over what had and hadn't worked. Not much fell into the second category. He didn't mention the pounding Gabriel had taken, but did vaguely warn against more 'mental breakdowns.'

As they gathered by the double doors leading back out to the field, Gabriel saw Ronnie corner the Coach again and make his point. In the crush, Gabriel was next to Tony Picarazzi. Gabriel smiled at him.

"Go easy on 'em in the second half, Tony," Gabriel said.

"No quarter," Tony said, and grinned.

But the kid who'd fumbled the kickoff for Milford at the end of the first half redeemed himself at the beginning of the second, taking it back eighty-eight yards for the touchdown to make it 41–13. Milford went for the two and, fired up, got it when their fullback pulled free from Gabriel and Ray's grasp and skidded into the end zone. That made it 41–15 and Gabriel did some math in his head on the sidelines: twenty-six points; four touchdowns, or three touchdowns with the two-point conversions and a field goal. He sat on the bench, unwrapping the tape on his wrists. Coach called him.

He ran over. "What's up?" he said.

"What's up?" Coach said. "Fixx, am I dreaming, or is the offense standing around out there on the field without a quarterback?"

He ran back to his spot on the bench, grabbed his helmet, and sprinted across the field to his teammates, buckling his helmet on the way.

"Glad you could make it," Andy said. "Run out of reading material?"

Gabriel looked at Ronnie, who wouldn't look back. The whole offensive line looked dangerous, Gabriel thought.

"Okay, look," he said. "Let's get another one and put an end to this, let some other people play."

That seemed pretty reasonable, he figured, coming out of the huddle. He was still congratulating himself when, backpedalling after the snap, he saw that no one had been blocked, that four defensive linemen and a blitzer to boot were pouring in on him like dogs on a thrown piece of meat. Like an idiot, he tried to complete the pass rather than just throw the ball away, and he paid for his decision.

He came back to the huddle with a sore shoulder, so mad he could hardly contain himself.

"Cut it out," he said. "Cut it out *right now.*"

"Cut what out?" Ronnie asked.

"Sorry about my man," Booth said. "He put a great move on me."

"Mine, too," Marcus said.

"What's going on here?" Pik asked.

"They're trying to get him killed," Andy said. He faced Ronnie. "You block for him, or I will personally kick your butt," he said.

"You'll kick whose butt?" Marcus said.

"Yours," Pik said.

"Awright, aw*right*," Gabriel yelled. It was his job to keep things together. "Nobody's gonna kick nobody's butt. And everybody's gonna do his job."

"Just call the play," Ronnie said.

Coach was signalling from the sidelines, mystified. He motioned to Gabriel: Did they need a timeout? Gabriel waved him off.

He called a play-action pass. He'd barely had time to execute the fake to Andy before he was on his back, Milford's middle linebacker on top of him.

Pik grabbed Marcus and spun him around.

"He was blitzing!" Marcus said. "What was I supposed to do? Wasn't he Kim's responsibility?"

Andy went for him, but Gabriel held him back.

"Come on, come on!" Gabriel shouted. He separated the two groups. To the offensive line he said, pointing, "You don't do your job on this play . . ." He trailed off, unsure how to finish the threat.

"Oh, I'm scared," Marcus said, bending into the huddle. Pik shoved him. Gabriel ignored them both, and called a pitch to Andy around Ronnie's side.

He watched Ronnie getting down to his three-point stance.

At the snap, Gabriel turned and pitched it perfectly to Andy, and then looked back at the line to see that Ronnie was somehow out of the picture, down in the tangle of bodies as if he'd never been standing. Andy was hemmed in by about seven Milford players, all frustrated at the beating they'd taken in the first half, and he ducked and curled, trying to protect himself, but he was buried.

Pik and Gabriel both pulled Ronnie out of the pile and to his feet, shaking him by the shoulder pads, ready to tear his head off. Marcus and Freed and Booth all jumped in, grabbing at them. One poor Milford player in the middle of it all, thinking that the two teams were fighting, took a swing at someone and missed.

Andy got up slowly, holding his knee. Coach called a timeout.

On the sidelines he asked, "What's going on?" Everyone was shouting at once, still hot. Coach asked again and, when they continued arguing, he figured that Pik and Gabriel and Marcus and Ronnie seemed to be the ringleaders, so he pulled them all. Johnson as a team wasn't that deep, and that meant some serious scrubeenies were going in; but what was Coach going to do, send everyone back out onto the field while they were still fighting?

He took them behind the bench, *"Now* what? Let's have some explanations!"

"They're laying down, Coach," Gabriel said. He felt like an informer but he couldn't help it. "They're laying down on their blocks and letting us get killed."

"We are not," Ronnie said.

"What are you saying?" Coach asked. "They're *intentionally* playing bad?"

"That's what he's saying, Coach," Pik said. Coach shot him a look. He already thought Pik was too wise for his own good.

"Why?" Coach asked. "Why would they do that?"

Gabriel hesitated. He thought about Tony Picarazzi, who didn't deserve to get dragged into all this. "I don't know," he finally answered.

"You don't *know*?" Pik yelped.

Gabriel shrugged, and gave Pik a warning look. Pik figured it out.

"*You* know?" Coach asked him.

Pik breathed out, hard. Then he replied, "No. Maybe they just don't like us."

"Maybe they just don't like you," Coach repeated, as if he were expected to believe that.

Everyone stood around, quiet. The offensive line looked pretty smug. Something happened on the field, and there was a roar from the Milford stands.

"Did it ever occur to you that these guys might be trying their hearts out?" Coach asked. He gestured at the offensive linemen, who looked forlorn. "That they may not have the gifts you guys have?" Gabriel could see he was working himself up to a righteous anger. "Did it ever occur to you that they don't need to hear you riding them every other play?" he said.

Pik was stunned. "But you were watching," he said. "Weren't you? Didn't you watch the last few plays?"

"I saw bad blocking," Coach replied. "Is that a crime? Is that enough to tear a team apart?"

Pik took his helmet off and held his palms over his eyes. Gabriel could see how much he was holding in.

"And you guys," Coach said to the offensive line. "You guys blocked like wimps out there on that last series. I'd be mad at you myself, if I were them."

"Yes, sir," Ronnie said in his worst kiss-up-to-the-adult voice. "We're going to give it our best once we get back out there."

"Yes you are," Coach said. "Or I'm going to rest you guys the way I'm going to rest these two here."

"Us?" Pik shouted. "You're benching *us*? After what *they* did?"

"That's the end of it, Telander," Coach said, and turned away. "The rest of you guys, get ready to go back in," he added over his shoulder as he left.

Gabriel restrained Pik from going after him. Ronnie, as he followed the rest of the offensive line back to the sideline, made a mincing good-bye wave with his fingers. Pik threw his helmet at him and missed. Ronnie kicked it farther down the sideline.

Ray DeVellis came over, the defense having come off the field. "What's going on?" he wanted to know, though it looked like he'd sort of guessed. They told him. Without a word, he turned and found Ronnie preparing to go in. Gabriel watched the two of them talk. He couldn't tell what Ray had said, but he saw that Ronnie looked more shook than he had when Gabriel and Pik had threatened him.

"What'd you say to him?" Gabriel asked when Ray returned.

28

Ray gave him a small smile. "My secret," he answered.

They looked at each other. "Hey, thanks a lot," Gabriel said to him.

"Yeah," Pik said, and Gabriel knew how difficult it was for Pik to say that: he was so enraged he could barely speak. "Thanks," Pik added.

"Something's gonna have to be done about this," Andy said. "Before the season's over."

"Before the next game's over," Gabriel said.

"In the meantime we sit here like jerks," Pik complained. He pushed over the Gatorade thermos. Some poor scrubeenie jumped back, his feet soaked by the wave.

And that was how the game ended: Pik and Gabriel on the bench, not quite believing it. The scrubeenies did okay. Tony Picarazzi had a good second half. Milford was blown out, 49–23. Andy, who was still in, took a beating. But it was always just one lineman, and always a different one, who missed a block, and it never seemed like anything you could prove. When the gun sounded ending the game, the three of them were alone on the bench. They refused to join in the celebrating. Too angry to move, too angry to do anything, they stared at their feet and imagined the showdowns — the private showdowns — that were to follow.

3.
Andy

What he wanted to do was kind of crazy. Andy knew that. Because what were those guys gonna do, admit they lay down on purpose? Then promise they wouldn't do it anymore?

But he couldn't think of any other way.

He was walking down the sidewalk, kicking stones with his Reeboks, testing his aching knee, thinking it over. This thing couldn't go on — someone was gonna get hurt bad. What if it was Gabriel, or Pik? Even if someone only had to miss a game or two, it was bound to cost them a win sooner or later; and they were too good to lose just because some guys didn't like some other guys. They were a *team*. They were the Maroon and Gold.

It was Saturday afternoon. Andy's father, a doctor, was at the hospital, as usual, and his mother — well, Andy didn't know where she was. He hadn't seen her in a long time; he could hardly remember her. She had left home when he was little. So Andy had been able to slip out of the house without telling anybody where he was going.

He'd made a couple of calls first, and he knew where to find everyone. They were all over at Ronnie Duggan's. It was just a few blocks from his house.

He'd never been there before, but he found it without difficulty. It was on a quiet street, a duplex facing a small park. Ronnie lived in the ground-floor apartment.

Andy walked up a few steps to the front porch and rang the bell. A tall woman wearing a beige dress opened the door. Andy introduced himself and asked if Ronnie was home.

"Why yes, he is," she said. "I'm Mrs. Duggan. The game's already started, but come in, I'll show you where they are."

She led him through the living room, through the warm kitchen smelling of food cooking on the stove, and down a short hallway. The sound of a sports announcer on TV grew louder.

"Right in there," Mrs. Duggan said, pointing.

He walked in and stopped and looked around. It was like he'd been dropped into the lion's cage at the zoo. Five or six of the linemen were crowded into the little room, sprawled on chairs, a day bed, and on the floor; they turned around to stare at him. In the background was the announcer saying, "Second-and-seven, and the Wolverines are going with a two-back offense . . ."

Mrs. Duggan's shoes clicked down the hallway, the sound fading.

Nobody said anything. Nobody looked at the TV.

They all stared at Andy.

Finally somebody said, "Have a seat, Kim."

Andy looked around. They were packed into the little room. There was nowhere to sit. And nobody moved over.

"No, that's all right," somebody else said, "just stand there for a couple of hours."

"Do a U-turn, why don't ya?" said Charlie Izzo, the center.

"Yeah," Lenny Marcus said, "do a one-eighty and keep going. Right back out the door."

"Okay, you guys," Andy said. He moved toward the TV, stepping over torsos and legs, and shut it off.

"Hey!"

"Yo, I'm watching that!"

"I wanna ask you something," Andy said when they quieted down. They were all there, he realized: all five linemen, and Tony Picarazzi, who gazed at him from the corner with an air of aloof interest.

"Sure, go ahead and ask," somebody said. "I really feel like answering."

"Listen," said Andy, "you think everybody doesn't know what you were doing? In the game last night. You think Coach won't know? That was stupid, what you were doing. You call that playing together?"

"Whatsa matter, Kim?" Ronnie Duggan interrupted. "You get hit last night?"

"Yeah," said Dave Booth. "Somebody tackle you?" He grinned, and showed his bad teeth.

"I don't mind taking a hit. The other backs don't either."

"It's dangerous out there; somebody might get hurt," Ronnie taunted.

"How come you carry the ball," asked Lenny Marcus, "if you're afraid to get hit?"

"Hey, guys, I hate to interrupt," said Lynn Freed from the floor, "but there's a game on here. Michigan-Notre Dame, remember?"

"It's all right," Andy said. "I know how it's gonna turn out. This is more important."

"Oh yeah?"

"What's the point, Kim?

"Get to the point."

"Your head, is that the point?"

"Turn the game on, Izzo," said Freed.

Andy yelled, *Hold it!*

They shut up.

"You were letting guys in last night. Falling down. Pretending to trip. You thought you were fooling everybody, but Coach'll know it pretty soon, just as soon as he sees the tapes of the game."

Andy had their full attention. The room was quiet.

He went on. "I came to tell you to cut it out! We could lose a game, you keep doing that. How can we win if we don't play together!"

From the chair in the corner, Tony Picarazzi passed gas. Everybody laughed.

Dave Booth said, "We won, Kim. So shut up."

"Hey Kim, hold it a sec," Ronnie Duggan said, sitting up. "You're saying we were letting guys in on *pur*pose?"

"Get serious, Duggan," Andy said. "You know you were."

Charlie Izzo, who'd been lying across the day bed with his huge shoulders supporting the wall, sat up, too. "Wait a minute," he said. "Let me get this straight. You're accusing me of letting my man in?"

"You all did."

"I say I didn't," said Izzo. "You calling me a liar?"

"You guys were like sieves last night."

Izzo said, "Answer my question. You say I let my man in on purpose?"

"Yeah."

"*I'm* saying, first," Izzo shouted, "my man got

in once, maybe twice, the whole game. Second, I didn't *let* the guy in. Now. Are you telling me I'm lying when I say that?"

"You know what I'm saying."

"Yeah, I know what you're saying. You're saying I'm sabotaging my own team *and* I'm a liar. Maybe you want to step outside and say that to me."

Andy thought it over. Charlie Izzo outweighed him by about forty pounds. Andy didn't think he'd mind fighting him too much, even if he lost, which was almost a certainty — he'd been beaten up before. But shoot, he'd come over here to patch it up, not to make it worse.

"Look, Charlie," Andy said, controlling himself, "and all you guys: I didn't come over here to pick a fight. All right? There's gotta be a better way to settle this and we've gotta settle it quick. We've gotta play together, we've — "

A chorus interrupted him: "Shut up!" "Sit down!" "Turn the game back on!" They were yelling and hollering at him. He heard footsteps outside the door, and then Mrs. Duggan stuck her head into the room.

"Everything all right in here, boys?"

"Just fine, Mrs. D."

"Yeah, great."

Ronnie got up and flicked on the television. "Say Mom," he said, "Andy was just leaving. Could you show him where the front door is?"

"Yeah," Izzo said, " 'less he wants to come outside with me."

Mrs. Duggan frowned — she seemed to know something funny was going on. Then she sort of shrugged and said pleasantly, "Come on, Andy. This way."

Andy, disgusted, turned and followed her.

Back at his house, Andy's doorbell rang not ten minutes after he got home.

He'd been thinking about what had happened at Ronnie's. He thought he'd probably made it worse. They'd admitted nothing, while he'd demonstrated that their tactics had gotten to him. That would only encourage them.

But worse, they probably considered him a chicken now: first for complaining about taking those hard shots in the game (*not* what he was complaining about) and, second, for refusing to go outside and fight.

The doorbell rang again before he got downstairs. Standing at the front door were Pik and Gabriel.

Andy let them in.

"Where've you been?" Pik asked.

Gabriel said, "We tried to call you but nobody answered."

Andy told them about his visit with the offensive line.

Gabriel said, "Oh, my my my."

Pik shook his head.

"You went over there alone?" Gabriel asked. "With your knee hurting like that?" He patted the top of Andy's head. "What's in there, mashed potatoes?"

"Charlie wanted to *fight* you?" Pik said. He laughed. "That gork. He's only about twice as big as you."

They went into the kitchen. Pik opened the refrigerator and looked inside.

"Hungry, Pik?" Andy said.

Pik closed the refrigerator door.

Gabriel was pacing around, shaking his head. "They didn't hate us last year because we didn't play that much. We were too little, too new to the team. We weren't a threat. Between the three of us this year, though, we're making about half the tackles."

"Yeah," Andy said, "and Ray's making all the rest of 'em."

"We're generating most of the offense, too," said Pik. "Right? It's either Kim turning the corner, or Fixx keeping the ball on a bootleg and picking up, oh, fifteen or twenty."

"Or Fixx throwing to Telander," Andy added.

"And where's Picarazzi in all this?" asked Pik.

"Yeah," Andy said, "Tony Picarazzi. Mr. Joe Montana last year, thirteen-for-forty-six and four interceptions, no touchdowns, and the team ends up below five hundred. So this year, we come along and Coach has us playing both ways and they're *not* happy!"

"We're also 1-and-0."

"Correct."

"We can't let them split this team," Gabriel said.

"This team could go all the way," Pik added.

Andy nodded. "Conference Championship."

"Who could beat us?" asked Pik.

There was a moment of silence.

Then all three of them spoke at once:

"Only Flood."

"The Blue and White."

"Scum-sucking preppies."

"You know it," Pik said, "and I know it."

"But does our offensive line know it?" Gabriel said.

"Do they care?" said Andy.

Pik slammed a palm on the counter. "They're going to ruin this team."

"What if one of us gets hurt?" Gabriel asked. "What if they pull the same deal next Friday and

Andy, say, has to leave the game? Or Pik? Or Ray?"

"We can't let 'em wreck the whole season," Pik said.

"Let's go back to Ronnie's house," Andy said eagerly, still upset that he'd turned down Izzo's challenge.

Gabriel grinned. "Uh, Andy? Do you really think that would help calm things down?"

Andy laughed. "I guess not."

"We need help," Pik said.

There was a silence. Then Gabriel said, "You think Coach has the tapes yet?"

Not much later they were knocking on Coach Kohut's door. He was home and told them the game tapes had just been dropped off. "Come in," he said. "I'll bet you're eager to see them."

Coach put the cassette in the VCR and rolled the tape. Watching the game on TV, Andy was disoriented at first by the angle of the shots, but he gradually began to recognize individual players wearing maroon and gold, some by their numbers, others by positions or moves.

The offensive line didn't look too bad. They played well during the first quarter, opening holes for Ray and him, and keeping the defensive line out pretty well on pass plays. But in the second quarter they began missing blocks. Just a few. Gabriel groaned as he watched himself get sacked, and Andy could tell that it was all Pik could do to keep from yelling at the flagrant errors of the linemen. But the bad plays mostly looked like confusion or missed blocking assignments or getting beat: honest mistakes.

Then, in the third quarter, Andy saw himself take a ferocious hit on an off-tackle play. He winced as he saw himself get creamed in the backfield by about seven guys.

Coach Kohut chuckled. "Wham! Oh boy, they socked it to you there, Kim. How did that one feel?"

" 'How *does* it feel?' you mean, Coach." Andy rubbed his ribs on the right side. "It hurts every time I breathe."

Coach replayed it. "Look there, see how Duggan slips on that play?" He fiddled with the remote and replayed it. "See? Right there!" He freeze-framed it with Duggan and Marcus falling down, and half the defense zeroing in on Andy.

"Come on, Coach," Pik said. "They can't stand us. They're doing that on purpose."

Coach gazed at them, his face hard. "What you're saying they did is pretty serious."

Pik nodded. "That's right, Coach. It's pretty serious."

Gabriel said, "This is the third quarter, right?

We had a big lead. You might've put Tony in sooner."

"What's this I'm hearing?" Coach asked.

"You could've played the back-ups sooner," Gabriel repeated.

Coach said, "I'm not hearing someone who doesn't want to play, am I?"

Gabriel shook his head. "Course not. I just want . . . I want things to be fair."

"Because if I thought for a minute," Coach continued, "that you didn't *want* to play, I'd bench you in a second."

Pik said, "But Coach, you don't understand. Those guys are a year older, and they — "

"Shut up!" Gabriel cut him off. "He understands fine."

Andy knew that Gabriel was trying to hold the team together by giving Tony more playing time. What he didn't know was why Gabriel didn't try to explain that to Coach.

Coach said to Gabriel, "You do have a point there, Fixx. There's some wisdom in taking you out, maybe preventing an injury, but only in the fourth quarter, not the third. You're our quarterback, and I want to give you as much playing time as I can without running up the score on a weak team. You need the experience. It'll come in handy later in the season, as the other teams improve along with us."

Coach turned his attention back to the TV. He fiddled with the remote, rewinding the tape and again reviewing the play on which Andy got creamed.

Watching it, Andy couldn't help wincing. His ribs throbbed.

"See there?" Coach said. "That was Duggan. Duggan and Marcus both missed blocks on that play. See how they slipped, how their feet just went right out from under them?"

"Coach," Andy said, "don't you remember what it was like out there?"

"Yeah, Coach," said Pik, unable to keep the bitterness out of his voice. "Remember that blizzard?"

"All that ice on the field?" Gabriel said.

Coach looked at them, eyebrows raised.

"Traction was good last night, Coach," added Andy. "Nobody was slipping around."

"Well, I don't know," Coach replied. "Doesn't look to me like they missed blocks on purpose."

Pik asked, "What're you, blind?"

There was silence in Coach's living room. Andy held his breath. He couldn't believe Pik had just said that. Gabriel gave Andy a look that said, *Let's get him outta here!*

Coach stared hard at Pik.

Pik, furious, stared back at him.

Gabriel stood up. Andy did, too.

But Pik and the Coach stayed put, their eyes locked.

Coach said softly, "You do have a lot of conviction on this, don't you, son?"

"I'm out there. I know these guys."

"Now, there's no reason to go and accuse me of being blind. Maybe you're right; maybe I am. Or maybe I just want to believe the best about the boys on my team." He shook his head, and looked up at Gabriel and Andy. "Go on, all of you. Film session's over. I'll see you at practice on Monday."

They left quickly. Outside, walking back to Andy's, Pik was outraged that Coach seemed unable to see what the line was doing. He said to Gabriel, "What's going on?" He turned to Andy. "And why didn't you tell him about what happened over at Duggan's?"

"What happened?" Andy said. "Nothing happened. They didn't even admit it."

"We can't say any more to Coach," Gabriel said. "It's our problem."

"That's right," Andy replied. "Coach'd just make it worse."

"If Coach went and told them to stop," Gabriel added, "those guys'd never let us live it down. We'd never win another game if Coach got on their case."

"I agree," Andy said. "We've got to cool it, try to work it out ourselves. See what happens in next week's game. That's the main thing. Pulling together during the game."

Pik looked at them as if they were both crazy. But he kept his mouth shut.

4.
Pik

Pik lifted Heinrich gently out of the big terrarium and cradled the scaly reptile in his right hand.

Heinrich was Pik's iguana. It was Sunday afternoon and Pik was fooling around in his room, alone. He was bored. There was nothing to do.

Crouching down in a three-point stance, Pik balanced Heinrich in his left palm and began to announce a football game in the voice of a TV sportscaster.

"Fourth-and-nineteen," he said excitedly. "The clock is winding down to eight seconds . . . seven . . . six . . . there may be time for Johnson to get one more play off, but they have to make it count — they're down by five points.

"And there's the snap! Fixx takes the ball and drops back. He looks to his left. He looks to his right."

Pik was standing now, his legs churning as though running.

"Down the right sideline, it's Telander to the twenty, to the ten. He's got a step on his man, and now the ball's in the air. It's spiraling down toward his outstretched hands through the haze and the lights, and Telander's in the end zone and the fans are on their feet!"

Pik leaped, his arm stretched all the way out, Heinrich balanced precariously in his palm. He flung himself across the bed, his other hand coming over to protect Heinrich as he bounced off the bed and onto the floor with a CRASH!

He hugged the iguana to his chest like a football.

"And he scores! Pik Telander has scored, ladies and gentlemen, and Johnson takes the game from Flood as the clock runs out!"

He lay on the floor, on his back, with Heinrich sitting on his chest, his shiny black eyes staring at him.

There was a knock on the door.

Pik hastily got up and sat on the bed. He set Heinrich down beside him.

"Come in?"

The door opened and in the doorway stood his father.

"What's up?" his father said.

"Nothing, Pop."

" 'Pop'?"

Pik shrugged.

"All that banging and crashing — I imagined it?"

"I was just hacking around. Playing a little Heinrich-ball."

"You be careful with that monster."

"Monster?"

"You heard it here first." His dad came into the room, ducking the model airplanes hanging from the ceiling, and sat down on the desk chair.

Pik slid back and leaned against the wall. Heinrich stayed where he was, crouched on the bed, still as a statue.

"Hey Pop," said Pik, "I've got a question for you."

His father raised his eyebrows. "Shoot."

"How do you make peace with a bunch of guys?"

"What do you mean?"

"Well, I mean if there's an argument over something. Bad feeling. How do you set things right?"

"That depends. You got a problem on the team or something?"

"Yeah, the football team."

Mr. Telander shrugged. "You might try talking to the guys you got a problem with."

"What if they don't want to talk?"

"Well then, you beat the daylights out of 'em." Pik's father laughed.

Pik didn't. "No, seriously."

"I don't know the guys, you know? So it's hard to say. Sometimes it helps to get a referee — sort of a go-between — to intervene for you. Mediate. You know?"

"I don't get it."

"What's this about, anyhow?"

"Nothing."

"Yeah, right." His father looked sideways at Pik.

Pik said, "See, there're these older guys on the team that Gabriel and Andy and I are starting ahead of — Gabriel even took the quarterback job away from one of the co-captains. And they played all last year and now their buddy, the quarterback, isn't playing, so they're blowing plays on purpose. Gabriel and Andy both got hammered last Friday."

Mr. Telander shook his head. "This is sports? This is friendly competition?"

"It's not *our* fault."

"Look at you." Pik's father waved his hand in Pik's direction. "You've been limping around here since last Friday because of that ankle. You've got a scab on your nose the size of a dime, and every time it begins to heal, somebody opens it up again for you."

Pik rubbed his nose. "But this doesn't have anything to do with that. I mean, this isn't *about* football. It's about these guys on the team who

. . . I don't know, they're worse than guys on the other teams. They don't even want to win. They'd rather get back at us."

"You think of talking to Coach Kohut about it?"

"We tried to. It came out during the game last Friday, but then Coach saw the tapes and didn't think anything was wrong. He's sort of naive — he doesn't believe anybody'd do such a dumb thing."

"Maybe he's just waiting it out. See if you guys can solve it yourself, without him stepping in."

"Gabriel thinks if Coach gets involved — the team'll just totally fall apart. And the other quarterback — Picarazzi's the kid's name — it isn't his fault."

"You agree?"

"With what?"

"With Gabriel? About your coach?"

Pik shrugged. "Maybe. He could have taken our word for it, when he looked at the tapes of the Milford game. But he saw it the other way, he said those guys just missed blocks."

"Well, maybe you ought to try talking to 'em then. Communicate. With the other guys, I mean. That's what it's all about: communication. Maybe they got something to say to you. Give 'em a chance to get it off their chests."

Pik looked at his father skeptically. "I don't know, Pop. Communication? Shoot, if Charlie Izzo has something to get off his chest, then I'd rather be in, you know, like Hartford, or Idaho. Someplace like that."

All week long, Coach Kohut worked them hard in practice. "You take it one week at a time," he told them, "one game at a time. Fairfield is coming down here on Friday to try to beat us at home, and they're tough this year. Very tough. They won their first game by a wide margin, just like we did. We got to be ready for them."

And all week long, the three of them argued about it: Pik wanted to talk to the linemen, Gabriel didn't, and Andy stayed neutral. In practice, Coach watched everybody closely, so there was no monkey business from the linemen: nothing was said, and nobody did anything outrageous or obvious. But the uneasy peace was more like a truce than a treaty, and contact sessions were mean and tense, with no talk, no laughter. Football was starting to feel more like nasty, hard work than fun.

Finally, Pik decided the heck with it, he'd just talk to 'em himself.

So one day after practice he hung around until Gabriel and Andy had taken off, and then he waded through the tape and towels strewn across the locker room floor, over to the corner where

Duggan and Picarazzi and the other linemen had lockers.

Ronnie Duggan was pulling a sweatshirt over his head.

"Hey, Ronnie, I want to talk to you," Pik said to the sweatshirt.

Ronnie's head popped out and swiveled around. His eyes focused on Pik. He looked surprised. "You want to talk? Talk."

"No, not here. Can we talk somewhere private?"

Ronnie's eyes narrowed. "You sure you want to talk?"

"That's all."

Ronnie shook his head. "Forget it. I've got to get home."

Pik said, "Home? What's the matter, you afraid just to talk?"

"Get serious, Telander. Okay, I'll meet you around back of the school. Ten minutes."

On his way out of the locker room, Pik walked past Ray DeVellis's locker. Ray was sitting on the bench in front of it, and he reached out and took hold of Pik's arm.

"What's going on?" Ray asked.

"Don't worry about it," Pik said.

Ray tightened his grip. "Where're Fixx and Kim?"

"They went home already."

"Where are you going?"

"It's okay," Pik said, pulling against Ray's grasp. "I can handle it."

Ray didn't look as though he believed him. But he let go of Pik's arm.

Outside, a cold wind whipped Pik's hair around. The sky was gray; the clouds were low and moving fast. It was beginning to get dark.

Pik's bad ankle had stiffened up after practice and, as he walked around to the rear of the building, he was limping. He sat down on the grass to wait. It wasn't long before they showed up, all six of them: Lynn Freed, Charlie Izzo, Ronnie Duggan, Tony Picarazzi, Lenny Marcus, and Dave Booth. They walked over to where Pik was sitting and formed a half-circle around him.

"So what's your problem, Telander?" Ronnie asked.

"Did I say I had a problem?" Pik said. "I must've forgotten I said that."

"You said you wanted to talk. All right. We'll listen. All of us."

"You hadda bring five guys out here just to listen to me?"

Charlie Izzo said, "You got a problem with that, Telander?"

Pik said, "It's not me that's got the problem. It's you, Izzo. And you, Duggan. All you guys.

You're wrecking the team, you and your problem."

"I don't have a problem," Duggan said. "You, Charlie?"

"Not me," Izzo said. "I ain't got no problem."

Duggan looked at Lynn Freed. "Got a problem, Lynn?"

Freed looked down at Pik, who was still sitting on the grass, trying to stay off his ankle. "Yeah," Freed said, "I got a problem. Some dog left it here, and I almost stepped in it."

"See," Duggan said to Pik, "you guys're just wise guys. You and Kim, and that kid who thinks he can play quarterback. You're just little punks. It's a problem, but not a big one."

Pik slowly stood up. He didn't weigh as much as the linemen, but he was taller than all of them except Picarazzi. "Do I look like a little punk to you, Duggan?" he said. "Do you want to make something of it?"

"I suppose you wanna fight, Telander. Is that right? You wanna fight?"

Pik snorted. "It wouldn't be fair, Ronnie. There're only six of you. Maybe you ought to go call a few more guys."

"That's it," Lynn Freed said, taking a step toward Pik. "I'm gonna do it right now. What do you say, Ronnie?"

Duggan shook his head and gave Freed the

thumb. The big lineman stepped back. "Tell your buddies to shape up," Ronnie said to Pik. "Talk to them, not to me. You and your two pals got a lot to learn."

"From who? You? How'd you guys do last year? I forget."

"Shut up!"

"You guys started this thing," Pik said. "You're wrecking our chances of winning."

"You gotta start showing some respect," Duggan said. "We're the older guys. You think you're hot spit, but you're not. You don't know your place."

Pik turned to Tony. "You know what's been going on, Picarazzi. Tell these guys to quit fooling around and play football."

Tony replied, "I never tell my offensive line what to do. I got no problem with you, Telander. Or with Fixx and Kim. But I am going to get my starting job back."

"That's up to Coach," Pik said. "Right? I mean, do I have anything to do with it? Does Fixx? And meanwhile, what about football? What about our team goals?"

"What sort of a team is it where one of the captains isn't playing?" Duggan said. "This isn't your team. It's ours."

"It's everybody's," Pik said. "And Coach plays

whoever he thinks is best. Best for the team, that is."

Lynn Freed stepped up to Pik. "Tony's best," he said, and he punched Pik in the face and knocked him down.

Pik got up and flew at him. He put his shoulder into Freed's gut and they both went down. As they grappled, Pik got hold of Freed's wrists and wrestled his way on top of him, then let go and started punching him in the face.

A couple of guys grabbed Pik and pulled him off Freed. Pik struggled, but they locked his arms behind him and held him while the big kid got up.

Freed's face was bleeding and he was breathing hard. He clenched his fists and started toward Pik.

Pik looked at Duggan, who was standing aside, watching. "Hey Ronnie," he said, "come on over and take a swipe at me yourself, instead of letting this animal do all your dirty work for you."

"Shut up," Freed said, cocking his arm.

Pik raised his leg and kicked at him. Freed caught his foot and twisted it.

Pik felt pain in his ankle where there already was pain. He screamed.

"That's enough!" Tony yelled.

The guys holding Pik dropped him. Pik lay on the ground, writhing, holding his ankle. It felt like it was on fire.

"Glad I'm not too late to join the fun." The voice, soft and menacing, came from behind him. Pik turned around.

There, by the corner of the building, stood Ray.

"Shove off, DeVellis," Duggan said. "This doesn't concern you."

"Now Ronnie," Ray said sweetly, "don't you remember what I told you during the Milford game?"

"Yeah, but — "

"I wouldn't forget it if I were you."

"We can finish this later, Telander," Duggan said, "if you and your two buddies don't start showing a little respect. DeVellis isn't always gonna be around to save your hide."

"Ronnie," Ray said, shaking his head.

Duggan looked at the ground.

"Go on," Ray said. "Get outta here. All of you. It's over."

"No it ain't," Freed said, wiping blood off his lip.

"Ronnie, I'm holding you responsible," Ray said. His voice sounded dangerous. "Get everybody out of here."

"Come on, guys," Duggan said. "Let's go."

One by one, they all turned and walked away.

Ray knelt over Pik. "How's the ankle?" he asked.

"Hurt," Pik said, rubbing it.

"Sorry I didn't get here sooner."

"No problem. I was handling it."

Ray laughed. "You were handling it, all right. That's why you were yelling at the top of your lungs, right?"

Pik grinned. He said, "What'd you say to Duggan, anyhow? At the Milford game."

"Can't tell you."

"Why not?"

"Just can't. Come on, it's getting cold." Ray gave him a hand up. They headed home, Pik leaning heavily on Ray's shoulder, limping.

Next day's practice — the last practice before the Fairfield game — was an easy workout, helmets and cleats but no pads. They warmed up, then ran through plays at full speed, no contact.

But Pik couldn't go full speed. His ankle was giving him real problems. Though it was heavily taped, it still felt funny. It was swollen and painful, and it made a sort of *click* when he ran. He didn't want to push it. It felt fragile as glass.

He talked with Gabriel about it on the sidelines, between drills.

"I still can't believe you went and got into a fight with Freed," Gabriel said. "After what Andy did the other day?"

"I just wanted to talk," Pik insisted.

Gabriel shook his head and chuckled. "Those

guys don't have vocabularies big enough to carry on a normal conversation."

"You're right," Pik said. "It was mostly grunting."

"Scratching themselves? Swinging from trees?"

Pik nodded. "Neanderthals, every one of 'em. Prehistoric. If Coach notices that I'm slower and takes me out . . ." He was too angry to finish the sentence.

Gabriel waited till he calmed down.

"Look," Pik finally said, "I'm going to play no matter what. Don't lead me as much. I'll be slower by a step or two."

"You'll have to rely on fakes, not speed, to get your guy off you," Gabriel reminded him. Then he shook his head. His hand snaked out and delivered a solid head-slap to Pik's helmet. "I only hope we don't get behind tomorrow," he said. "I only hope we don't have to go deep."

5.
Gabriel

Co-captains Tony Picarazzi and Ronnie Duggan, their home whites fresh and sparkling in the stadium lights, walked out onto the midfield stripe and lost the coin toss. Fairfield deferred the choice to the start of the second half, and Johnson elected to receive.

Gabriel pulled on his Riddell and trotted onto the field behind Andy, who turned and grinned at him.

"I got this one," Andy said.

"Bull," Gabriel countered. "Watch my cleats."

The two of them stood on the five-yard line and waited for the kick. Gabriel felt good — he felt ready. He always felt good once the real thing got underway.

The kick was high and deep, but it went to Andy's side of the field. As Andy planted himself under it, Gabriel drifted over in front of him and watched the players form downfield. He saw more of Johnson's white jerseys to his left and fewer of the Fairfield light blue, so when Andy shouted "Go!" he took off to the right and then, three or four steps later, cut sharply to his left. A hole opened up, a blue shirt filled it, and Gabriel spun his body at the guy's knees. The contact was so satisfying that Gabriel sat up laughing. From that position he watched Andy dance down the left sideline and go in for the score.

They huddled briefly before attempting the extra point — all business, no celebrating — and Gabriel said, "Nice blocking, guys. Let's do it again, on two." And somebody said, "Yeah, right," and somebody else said, "Eat it."

They broke the huddle and Charlie Izzo's snap was perfect; Andy kicked it up and through.

Gabriel tried to shake off what just happened. Was he hearing things?

While Andy was kicking off to Fairfield, Gabriel found Pik on the bench. Pik was off by himself, his helmet sitting high up on the back of his head.

"How's the ankle?" Gabriel asked, sitting down.

"It's okay."

"I saw you throw a block out there."

Pik shrugged.

"You got any speed at all?" Gabriel asked.

"Enough," Pik said. "If it's bad, I'll take myelf out."

Gabriel nodded, then gave Pik's thigh guard a hard slap and stood up. "First down," he said. "Let's hold 'em."

From their own twenty-five, Fairfield tried the middle a couple of times and found out that Ray could play middle linebacker. Then they threw an incomplete pass. They punted on fourth-and-eight, and Andy ran it back to the Johnson forty-five — good field position.

In the huddle, Gabriel called a quick slant-in to the wide receiver, but Pik was slow getting across the middle and Gabriel led him by too much. The ball was almost picked off downfield by the free safety.

Gabriel called a sweep around the strong side. Ray, leading the interference, flattened the cornerback and Andy picked up a first down in Fairfield territory. On the next play, Gabriel sent Ray off tackle, but Ray picked up only two when Ronnie Duggan's man got a clear shot at him.

Gabriel knelt down in the huddle but, before he could say anything, Pik said, "Let's go, Duggan, block somebody."

"Shut up, Telander," Duggan said.

Gabriel said, "Both of you shut up," and called a sweep to the weak side. As the huddle broke he thought he saw a look between Booth and Freed, but he shook it out of his mind.

As the play developed, the right side of the line caved in and Andy was tackled for a three-yard loss.

That made it third-and-eleven.

In the huddle, Pik said, "Hey Freed, try holding the guy. Maybe that'll work."

Charlie Izzo reached across and yanked on Pik's face mask, and Pik shoved him.

"Cut it out!" Gabriel yelled as the two struggled.

Ray's voice silenced everyone. "Let's take a little pride in ourselves here," he said quietly. "Take it out on the other team."

From the sideline, they could hear Coach Kohut hollering: "What's going on out there? Let's go, call a play!"

Gabriel called Pik's number and said, looking up at the angry faces around the huddle, "Come on now, give me some time, we need this first down."

But he never even had a chance to set up. As he backpedalled away from center, he watched in amazement as the entire offensive line — five guys — fell backward and four Fairfield players, their blue jerseys luminescent in the stadium lights and their eyes gleaming in eager anticipation, bore down on him. He tucked the ball away and tried to split two of them, but they hit him high and low as if they'd planned it that way. A bright light flashed behind his eyes.

When he sat up, there was a ringing in his ears and his vision was blurred. He saw players streaming on and off the field and someone leaned over and offered his hand. It was Andy.

"What down is it?" Gabriel asked as Andy pulled him to his feet.

"Fourth," Andy said.

Gabriel knelt down in the middle of the huddle and looked around at faces he barely recognized. He tried to think of a play, but nothing came into his head.

"Ummmm," he said. "Uhhhh . . ." His eyes focused on Andy.

Andy looked concerned. "We're punting," he said. "On one."

The huddle broke and Gabriel heard Andy say to him, "Just call the signals."

He did and Andy punted it away cleanly. Gabriel headed downfield looking for the guy with the football and never saw the kid who blocked him.

The other team wound up with good field position. Gabriel couldn't remember who they were playing. Milford? Flood? He played defense on autopilot, flowing with the movement of the players in front of him, looking for anyone in a blue jersey to tackle or cover.

Andy came over to him once and asked him if he felt all right.

"Why're you asking?" Gabriel said.

"You just tackled their wide receiver," Andy said.

"Yeah, I know," said Gabriel.

Andy looked at him funny. "The guy didn't have the ball," he said. "It cost us fifteen yards."

After the next play, Gabriel took himself out of the game.

As Tony Picarazzi trotted onto the field buttoning his chin strap, Coach came over to Gabriel.

"What is it, son? What's wrong?"

"I'll be all right, Coach. I'm a little dizzy."

"Okay, relax. Take it easy." Coach patted his shoulder pad and went away.

Gabriel sat on the bench, watching the game. He was thinking hard, but he just couldn't. . . . Then suddenly he remembered: Fairfield. They were playing Fairfield.

Immediately he felt better.

They were in the second quarter now, and Fairfield was keeping the ball on the ground, not making mistakes, grinding out a few yards here, a few there. They didn't make big plays, but they kept making first downs, and finally the score was tied. When they kicked the extra point, they tied it.

Gabriel went out to receive the kickoff with

Andy, but when Fairfield put it in the air, Gabriel saw two footballs coming toward him and couldn't decide which one to catch. While he was making up his mind, Andy cut in front of him, caught the ball at full speed and headed upfield. He got to his own thirty-five before several blue jerseys wiped him out.

Gabriel jogged off the field, helmet in hand, and shook his head at Coach, who gave Tony Picarazzi some last-minute instructions and sent him in to run the offense. Gabriel sat down despondently to watch.

The team went nowhere, punted, played some good defense, and got the ball back. A couple of downs later, Tony underthrew Pik and a Fairfield linebacker intercepted.

Gabriel hung his head; he could not believe that Picarazzi could throw the ball *behind* the hobbled Pik. Couldn't he — Gabriel — do better than that? Even seeing double?

The interception gave Fairfield the ball on Johnson's thirty-seven. Johnson held them for a couple of downs but, on third and long, their halfback broke through the defensive line, juked Tony so bad he fell down, and headed down the sideline toward the end zone. Andy saved it with a diving tackle just inside the ten.

But it wasn't enough. Three plays later, they

scored again. That was how the half ended: Fairfield 14, Johnson 7.

The first thing Coach did at halftime was take Gabriel aside and ask him how he felt.

"I think I can play all right, Coach."

"No, I mean, how do you *feel*?"

"I feel all right. I just can't — " He hesitated. It would sound ludicrous.

"What?"

"I can't remember the plays."

"Can't remember the plays? You mean you can't remember what to do?"

"No. I can't think 'em up. I can't remember their names."

Coach called the trainer over. The trainer was an older man with white hair and large, calloused hands. He looked into Gabriel's eyes and said, "You've had your bell rung."

"Very perceptive observation," Gabriel muttered.

The trainer told him to hold his head still and follow his hand with his eyes. He waved his hand back and forth in front of Gabriel's face.

Gabriel watched the hand without moving his head.

"He'll be all right," the trainer said to Coach Kohut.

The Coach said to Gabriel, "What if I call the

plays from the sideline? Could you execute?"

"I think so."

"You could remember what to do?"

"Yeah."

"Okay, we'll do it that way. And Picarazzi'll play defense for you."

In the third quarter, losing by seven, the Johnson defense bent, but did not break. Fairfield drove down inside the twenty, then fumbled the ball away. Three downs later, Andy punted it back to them; they drove all the way back, stalled at the twenty-two and missed a field goal.

After that, Johnson was able to move the ball against Fairfield by a combination of sweeps and short passes: Fixx to Telander, and Fixx to Kim. But with this success, the mood got ugly. In the huddle, there was mouthing off and shoving while they waited for plays to come in from the sideline. Andy and Pik had words with the linemen.

Gabriel was feeling okay: his head hurt, but the dizziness and weakness were gone. He was passing crisply and pitching out with accuracy. He was getting blocking, and that was all he wanted: he didn't care who said what to whom, as long as everyone played hard and did their job. But as they approached the Fairfield ten-yard line, the team's momentum disintegrated.

It was third-and-four. Gabriel took the snap and

rolled to his right, looking to throw to Andy out of the backfield, and suddenly the whole right side of the line caved in when Booth and Freed both missed their blocks. He threw the ball high and far — out of bounds, he thought — and braced himself. He was running flat out, full speed when one guy hit him low. He fell, and saw the ground coming up at him.

The next thing he knew, he was looking up at Ray and a couple of other players, who were bending over him.

What happened? he wondered. *I must've blacked out for a few seconds. . . .*

As Ray helped him up, Gabriel saw Andy limping off, supported by the trainer and a player.

"What happened to Andy?" Gabriel asked.

"Knee," Ray answered.

"Oh man," said Gabriel. "What next?"

"Exactly," replied Ray.

Gabriel leaned on Ray all the way to the sideline, then made it back to the bench by himself as Ray and Tony headed out onto the field. He found Andy and sat down next to him.

They looked at one another.

"Are you all there?" Andy said.

"Why?"

"Your eyes are looking in two different directions."

"Why do you think I've got two of 'em?" He thought about that. "Don't I?"

Andy said, "What're you doing here, anyhow? I thought you played football."

"I'm missing a few minutes," Gabriel answered. "They got lost. How come we've got the ball?"

"You took us all the way down there. I was gonna score. Then you threw one at the moon."

Gabriel asked, "What happened to your knee?"

"I go up for that so-called pass you threw," Andy said, "and I'm coming down, and I land on this leg here just as some guy comes along and tries to remove it from my body."

Gabriel shook his head, but quickly stopped when the bench dipped and he almost fell off it.

Things began to come back to him gradually. "They did it again," he said. "They just lay down. I was gonna be sacked, so I threw it away."

"It's okay." Andy shrugged. "It wasn't your fault." He turned and looked over his shoulder, at the stands.

Dazed, Gabriel watched as Picarazzi tried to run the offense. They were very close to a score.

Andy sat beside him, holding his knee and occasionally looking over his shoulder at the stands.

"What's going on back there?" Gabriel finally asked. But he didn't turn around — he was afraid he'd fall off the bench.

"I was just looking for my father," Andy said. "He was gonna come, maybe. But I don't think he made it. That's one good thing — he didn't see me get hit in the knee again."

They both turned their attention back to the game. On the field, Picarazzi almost fumbled the snap on third down. He missed the hand-off and was tackled for a two-yard loss. So they went for a field goal on fourth down, and Picarazzi, filling in for Andy, put up a chip shot that barely stayed within the uprights.

It was 14–10, and there was a whole quarter of football to play.

With Picarazzi at quarterback, Coach Kohut continued to call the plays. He mixed in a few passes with the run, but it didn't work: Tony completed only one short pass. Ray would pick up a few yards every time he ran the ball, but the second-string tailback, in for Andy, couldn't remember his assignments, and Tony kept having to eat the ball.

The good news, though, was the Johnson defense: they stopped everything Fairfield threw at them, even without the starting safeties out there. That was mainly because Pik and Ray, facing a loss for the first time this season, had raised the level of their game, so Fairfield had difficulty getting the ball beyond the line of scrimmage.

Because they were ahead, they didn't pass much, and their running game was getting stuffed by Pik and Ray, who were everywhere: Pik, though slowed by his ankle, spent most of his time in the opponent's backfield, and Ray stopped up the middle, then moved to his right or his left to string the sweeps out to the sideline. Because of Ray's pursuit and Pik's ability to jam up a play, the Fairfield backs never had a chance to turn the corner and head upfield.

Still, the final quarter was rapidly dwindling away; with both teams sticking to the ground, there weren't a lot of incomplete passes bouncing around to stop the clock. So when Tony Picarazzi fumbled a punt on the Johnson fifteen-yard line with only 3:45 left, the game appeared to be lost, even though Tony leaped on the ball and recovered it.

Gabriel wondered why Coach wasted a timeout at this point, and when he called the entire offense over to the sideline, he figured he was giving them one more pep talk. Andy got up and went over to the huddle, and Gabriel got up, too — he wanted to hear what Coach had to say — but the field tilted strangely, nearly knocking him over, so he quickly sat down again.

When Andy returned, Gabriel asked what had gone on in the huddle.

Andy said, "Coach told 'em to pull out all the

71

stops. He said he was going to give the ball to Ray, that it was up to Ray to win the game. He said he thought Fairfield was gonna be surprised." Andy gave a shrug.

"Yeah," said Gabriel, "they'll be surprised all right. They'll be surprised if somebody blocks for him."

"So will I," added Andy.

True to his word, Coach Kohut started sending in Ray's number on every play. Fullback off tackle. Fullback up the middle. Fullback draw. Quick opener to the fullback. Ray picked up three yards, seven yards, four yards, five yards, thirteen yards. From the bench, Gabriel could see the sweat dripping off his chin; he could see Ray struggling between plays to get his breath back.

Tony spun and tucked the ball away in Ray's gut, pulled it out, backpedaled and set up, then tossed a little flare pass and Ray caught it and turned upfield. Gabriel saw one defender bounce off Ray's thigh and another grab at his shoulder pad and slip off. Gabriel thought he might go all the way, but he was caught from behind and dragged down.

First-and-ten at the Fairfield thirty-five and Ray slashed off-tackle. The blocking was terrible, but Ray accelerated and slipped between two big linemen, then stiff-armed a linebacker. And when one of the cornerbacks finally hit him low and hard, Ray spun and fell forward for two extra yards. On the next play he got outside and turned the corner, and Gabriel saw one safety bounce off him, and then the other shoved him out of bounds, stopping the clock.

Ray didn't make guys miss tackles, Gabriel was thinking: he just didn't go down easily. He wouldn't juke you; you'd hit him and just bounce off. It wasn't his speed but his power and his reliability — the fact that he hardly ever fumbled. And Ray had stamina. He could go on running and taking punishment and return to the huddle and get his wind and strength back and be able to accelerate and break tackles on the very next play, and the next, and the next. . . .

And it didn't appear to matter that he wasn't getting any support from the line. It seemed to Gabriel that the line had already quit, that they were only going through the motions. The best thing about how they were playing was that they weren't getting in DeVellis's way.

Ray came out for a breather on first down with the ball near the fifteen-yard line. Coach tried the substitute tailback and then he tried a quarterback draw. He sent Ray back in on third and nine and Ray took the handoff but got hemmed in by two defenders. Without cutting back — just by changing speed with a little stutter-step — he got past those two, broke two more tackles and picked up twelve.

On the next play, he scored.

The entire bench stood as one — in awe of what Ray had done.

Tony Picarazzi missed the extra point, and there was a collective groan from the stands: Johnson was only up by two, 16–14. A field goal would beat them.

But just seventeen seconds remained, and a weak kickoff return and three pass attempts later, Fairfield ran out of luck. And time. During a fourth-down play, the clock ticked down to double-zero, and Johnson had won.

Only the benchwarmers and the people in the stands celebrated. The game had taken its toll on the starters — they looked as though they were returning from battle. Their white jerseys were now gray and sweat-soaked, their hair was dripping wet and matted down, their faces and arms were streaked with dirt and blood.

Still, it had not really been a team victory. It was a miracle attributable mainly to one player: Ray DeVellis.

Pik came over, sat down on the ground near Gabriel, and leaned exhaustedly against the bench.

Ray wandered by and collapsed close to Pik

and Gabriel and Andy. He lay there breathing hard, but otherwise not moving, his eyes closed, his hands folded across his chest like a cadaver.

Gabriel could tell that Ray was totally exhausted and didn't have the energy to celebrate. Glad they'd won, but glad it was over, too.

People streamed past: parents, sisters and brothers, classmates, everyone in a jubilant mood after the victory. . . .

Except the four of them: Ray, Gabriel, Andy, Pik.

What was to celebrate? Key guys were injured, the team was in disarray, and most of the season was still ahead of them.

6.
Andy

Andy had been Mr. Shake-It-Off around the guys, but his knee injury scared him, a lot, and now he had no one to talk to about it. He'd felt something go when he'd come down on it. He'd heard a little, almost internal *crick* — as if he'd heard it with his bones instead of his ears — just like a walnut, and it had scared him down to the soles of his feet. The team trainer had checked it out after the game, swiveling his leg this way and that, as casually as if he were handling a hose or a piece of rope. He'd pronounced it all right. But what did *he* know? He was the one who'd looked into Gabriel's eyes and told him he'd just had his bell rung. No kidding. Gabriel had spent the second half wandering around like someone just in from *The Planet of Lost Souls*.

Andy was no wuss, but he knew what he was capable of, and he was no longer sure the knee would stand up to serious cutting, to all of his weight moving across it. And playing halfback and returning kicks was not going to work without lateral movement.

So he spent the afternoon on his living room sofa, his knee elevated on a pillow on the coffee table. He just sat there. The TV was on. Some incredibly stupid movie involving kung fu guys.

The good news was that his father was a doctor, so he wouldn't be in the dark too long.

The bad news was that his father didn't want him playing in the first place. So Andy was terrified that he'd take one look at the knee and announce that Andy's playing career was over. Either because it *was* over — and Andy shook that thought right out of his mind as too terrible even for even someone as paranoid as he was — or because his father said it was.

Well, Andy didn't have to tell him. Given the amount of time he saw his father lately, it might be all healed before his father noticed anything.

He snorted. Given the amount of time he saw his father lately, he might be off to college before his father noticed anything.

His father was supposed to have been home at six o'clock. It was now seven-thirty. Andy had made cube steaks. He'd left them in the oven and had turned the broiler off. By now they were stone cold, little pieces of shoe leather.

This happened a lot. Andy's father was a good doctor, and took his work very seriously. And so, of course, he was always busy and always coming home late. It made sense. What was he supposed to do, walk out on sick people? Tell them he understood that they were in trouble, but that he was supposed to be home and chowing down at a certain time?

Meanwhile, Andy came home and cooked as if his father were going to show up.

The kung fu guy kicked someone in the face, extending his leg and lashing out like a Rockette. Andy winced just seeing the guy's knee do that. He lifted his bad knee higher and bunched up the pillow.

The more he thought about it, the more he thought the whole idea of having his father look at the leg was a bad one. No matter how okay it was, his father was not going to like the idea of his playing on it, this season or any season, and Andy was just going to catch endless grief.

He could picture his Dad standing there, arms folded, Mr. Reasonable: *Andy, there are only so many hours in the day, and football takes up too many of them. Remember, the key is not letting your studies slide. Do you know how few people get to play at the college level?* And Andy would reply, *But Dad, my grades are good.* His father would then say, *Imagine what they could be if you concentrated on nothing but your studies?*

Andy sighed loudly, sounding like the guy with

the dubbed voice in the king fu movie. Who needed the hassle?

He heard the sound of his father's car in the driveway, and then the garage door. There was a bumping at their front door, and his father came into the house. Andy could hear him putting things down in the kitchen and then calling out a tired hello. Andy called one back, and said he was in the living room. His father came in and nodded to him, heading upstairs.

"I'm beat," his father said. "Twelve hours today, and yogurt for lunch."

"There're cube steaks in there," Andy said as his father trooped up the stairs.

"I'm too tired," his father replied from the top of the landing. From his bedroom he said, "Maybe in a little while. You eat?"

"Yeah, I had mine," Andy said, though he hadn't. He was hungry, too. Why he did stuff like that, he had no idea.

Upstairs there was the sound of his father's shoes hitting the floor, and the creak of the bed. The closet door opened and shut. He heard the sound of metal hangers.

He took his leg off the pillow, and sat with both feet on the floor. He threw the pillow over onto the recliner.

His father came back downstairs in his robe, a ratty blue terrycloth number, as if he were sick himself. He passed back through the living room on the way to the kitchen. "How was your game?" he asked.

"We won," Andy said. "16–14."

"Good," his father said. He was at the sink in the kitchen, letting the water run to get cold.

Andy watched the movie. His father came out and sat in the recliner, giving the pillow a look before tossing it onto the sofa. He settled in and took a long drink from his water glass. He looked around the room and peered at the movie. Finally he said, "What's this?"

"Some stupid kung fu movie or something," Andy said.

"You're watching this?" his father said. "Shouldn't you be doing your homework?"

Andy got up. He felt a twinge in his knee, and flexed it out straight carefully. He walked off, a little stiffly.

"Beat up, huh?" his father said.

"Yeah," Andy said. "Beat up."

"If you quit football you'd have more time to watch things like this, and still get your homework done," his father said. He was already changing the channel with the remote.

"Yeah," Andy said. "Look what I'm missing."

He hobbled up the stairs. His father looked over once while Andy was on his way up and said, "You *are* beat up." When Andy stopped, his father said,

"Is your leg all right? Want me to look at it?"

"It's okay," Andy said.

"If you want me to look at it, let me know," his father said. Then he returned his attention to the TV.

Andy decided on a hot bath even though ice might have been better, and lay in it for a while, his leg feeling less painful. It still looked swollen. He slumped down so that his nose was underwater and his eyes above, imagining himself an alligator out for prey.

He lay there in the hot water and thought about the offensive line having done this to him. If they'd blocked, Gabriel wouldn't've had to throw such a bad pass, and he wouldn't've had to spread himself out like that going after it. They'd hurt Pik, they'd hurt Gabriel, and now they'd hurt him. He got enraged just thinking about it. And here he'd backed off on fighting them. He should've gotten a shovel and gone after all of them. Suppose he'd done some permanent damage to his knee? He'd tried to be nice, he'd tried to be reasonable, and how far had it gotten him?

He lay there and tried not to think about practice the next day, about cutting on the knee, about having it planted when people hit him, even at half-speed. His forehead started sweating, and he dunked himself under the water. With his head submerged he could hear that little noise again, that *crick*, in his memory, and he slapped the water surface with his fist, sending a wave up the tile wall.

He showed up late for practice, hoping Pik and Gabriel would already be busy out on the field, but naturally they'd waited around for him. They were standing there on the sidelines horsing around. He could see that he wasn't going to get out of this easily.

"Glad you could make it," Pik said when he walked up.

"Thanks for stopping by," Gabriel said. He gave Andy a shove and Andy made a little exaggerated hop to stay off the knee.

"Watch it, watch it," he said, trying to explain himself. "I'm trying to go easy on the knee."

"Still a little sore, huh?" Pik said. He was looking out over the field, anxious to get out there.

"Not so sore," Andy said. He leaned on and off it experimentally. It didn't feel a hundred percent. To tell the truth, it didn't feel seventy percent.

"You're not worried about it, are you?" Gabriel said.

"What'd your father say about it?" Pik asked. He was strapping his helmet on.

"My father?" Andy said.

Gabriel looked at him. "You remember your father. The guy you live with? The doctor?"

Andy got busy attaching the chin strap to his own helmet, snapping and resnapping the four straps. "I didn't tell him," he said.

When he looked up, both Pik and Gabriel were staring at him. "You didn't tell him?" Gabriel asked.

"If you guys have had your social hour, it'd be nice if you could join us at least for the last few minutes of our activities out here," Coach called from the middle of the field. He made an exaggerated bow. "Gentlemen?"

Pik and Gabriel were still waiting for Andy to explain. Gabriel nodded to Coach and waved, like they'd soon be on the way. That was a move, Andy thought, that wasn't going to endear the three of them to Coach. And as if they weren't in enough trouble to begin with.

Andy said, "I was worried. I was worried he'd tell me I had to stop playing."

The three of them were quiet. Gabriel put an arm around him. He said, "Is the knee all right?"

Andy felt almost like crying. Talk about your wusses, he thought. He replied, "I don't know."

"All right, well, practice is as good a place as any to find out," Pik said. "We'll just take it easy, and see how you feel."

"Gentlemen!" Coach called again, exasperated.

They ran out onto the field. Gabriel apologized. Pik explained that Andy's knee was giving him problems, and wondered if he could just walk through things, while he tested it out.

"How bad is it?" Coach asked. "You wanna have it looked at at the medical center?"

Very much, Andy thought. "No, it's all right," he said.

"Tough it out," Coach said. "Is there a lot of instability?"

"Nah, it's fine," Andy said, pivoting a little to demonstrate. *Idiot*, he thought. *Jerk. Go have it looked at.*

That was the end of that. Practice resumed. On defense Andy ran through some of the coverages for the safety-valve options for the halfback. He did everything gingerly. He was finishing up one play when he felt a jolt from behind, and turned to see Ronnie Duggan, grinning at him.

"Watch that knee," Duggan said. Andy felt a chill like the kind you get during a horror movie.

"Enough already with the run-throughs," Coach said. "Let's try some full contact here." Most of the guys groaned, while Coach clapped his hands. Duggan looked over at Andy and pointed, and mouthed something Andy couldn't make out through the face mask.

Back in the loose practice huddle of the defense, Andy didn't know what to do. He said to Pik, in a voice he hoped didn't sound too panicked, "They're gonna go after my knee."

"Who is?" Pik asked. Then he knew what Andy was talking about.

Gabriel said, "They're not going to do that." He gave Andy what he thought was an encouraging nod.

"What're we talking about here?" Ray wanted to know.

"More trouble," Pik said.

"I doubt it," Ray said. Andy didn't know whether he meant he'd prevent it, or that there was no trouble to worry about in the first place.

Some of the other guys in the huddle wanted to know what the heck everybody was talking about. But by then the offense was lined up and ready, so Gabriel shut everybody up and they broke and took their positions.

Tony Picarazzi started calling the signals. From his stance, Duggan said, "Fresh meat at free safety." And Lynn Freed said "Rowrf, rowrf, rowrf."

At the snap, Duggan fired out past Pik, like it wasn't his job to block the defensive end, and headed toward Andy. Pik spun, caught him from behind, and wrestled him down. Freed also took off for Andy, but never got there, blindsided by Ray. The play, of course, completely disintegrated. It looked like chaos out there. Duggan and Freed both got up swinging.

"Hold it, hold it, hold it!" Coach yelled. "What the heck was *that*?"

"The guy's tackling me," Duggan complained. Everyone was yelling at once.

Coach waded in and separated everyone. He reamed them out as a group. Pik opened his mouth to say something and Coach said, "Telander, you start again with your conspiracy theories and you'll be sitting out a lot more than this practice."

Pik clammed up.

He asked what was going on, and this time no one would say anything. They all just stood there. Andy thought, *This is so stupid*, and wanted to scream.

Coach finally gave up. "All right, let's try no-contact again," he said.

So they did, running through most of their plays that way. Everyone avoided hitting or even brushing into one another, as though even the slightest contact might kick off a huge free-for-all. Then Coach assembled the starting offense, and decided to have it run its plays at full speed with no defense at all to worry about. Those not starting on offense were sent off the field. They lounged around near the Gatorade bucket and sprawled on the grass.

This is it, Andy thought. This was where he'd find out about his knee one way or the other. The first play was a straight drop-back pass with both backs in, so all he had to do was come up out of his stance into a blocking position, to help out with the pass rush. That was no problem. But the second play Coach called was a 39 Slant, with the halfback expected to come out of the backfield as the primary receiver, make a sharp cut at the sidelines, and cross the field diagonally to lose the linebacker in coverage.

It would've been hard to pick a worse play, in terms of a strain to his knee.

Coming out of the huddle, Gabriel must have seen Andy's eyes, because he said, "Don't worry about it. Take it easy, and you'll be fine."

He did, and he was, though his cut was slow enough that even Coach noticed.

"C'mon there, Kim," he called. "We need a little more speed than *that*. Is the knee giving you that much trouble?"

So they ran the play again, and Andy decided to crank it up, though not to full throttle. When he made the cut, his knee buckled like Jell-o, and down he went.

He flopped around on the grass, scared. Pik and Gabriel and Coach hustled over to stand next to him. He flexed the knee to make sure he hadn't done any more damage.

"That's it for you today," Coach said. He waved in Mike MacDonald. Pik and Gabriel helped Andy to the sidelines, just to be safe. Duggan and all those guys on the offensive line were standing around with their hands on their hips watching. They didn't look particularly sympathetic, but they didn't look particularly satisfied, either. It was as if an injury that they hadn't caused was no reason to celebrate.

Andy was stuck just watching, and worrying about his knee. And on top of everything else, the team wasn't executing particularly well. Coach got frustrated and kept them later than usual. It seemed to Andy that he sat there on the sidelines flexing his knee and watching everybody else run around for weeks, months, years. People would come over to the Gatorade bucket for a drink and nod at him sympathetically until he got to feeling like someone's great-grandfather in an old folks' home. He almost got up and left a few times. It turned out to be the hardest practice of his life, for all the wrong reasons.

Toward the end of it, Duggan came over, soaked in sweat and puffing his cheeks like someone playing the bugle. He poured himself some Gatorade and squatted next to Andy, peering at him while he drank.

"How's the knee?" he finally asked. Andy couldn't tell how he meant it.

"All right," Andy said warily.

"Doesn't look all right," Duggan said. "If it's all right, why aren't you in there?"

"It'll be all right for Friday night," Andy said.

Duggan didn't say anything. He was looking out over the field, where the guys were standing around, taking advantage of Coach's indecision about whether or not to run a play again.

Andy felt as if he should talk, as if he had a chance here to use his knee to patch things up.

"Look. Let's just forget this whole thing happened," he said.

Duggan looked over at him for a long minute. Andy had the fleeting feeling that he'd succeeded, that their problems were over.

"Let's not and say we did," Duggan said.

Andy stared at him. Duggan stood up and strapped his helmet back on.

"Why?" Andy said.

"Oh, yeah, poor Kim hurt his knee so we should forget all of this," Duggan said.

Andy could feel himself reddening. What he hated most was having manuevered himself into a position where Duggan, of all people, was right.

"Get away from me," Andy said. "I don't even know why I bothered talking to you."

Duggan threw the cup away and smiled at him. "Watch that knee," he said, leaving.

Gabriel and Pik came over, under the pretext of getting Gatorade. "What was that all about?" Gabriel asked, while Pik filled his cup.

"I was just doing our cause some good," Andy

said disgustedly. What angered him even more was that, once again, he'd seemed like a wuss, a wimp, for trying to be reasonable.

"I think we're going to have to just give up on Duggan," Pik said.

"Not as long as he's blocking for us we're not," Gabriel said. "We're still a team. And I'm still running it."

"Maybe so," Pik added. "But let me tell you something, team leader. If he gets anybody else hurt, or goes after Andy, or anything else, I'll personally take off my helmet and beat him to death with it."

"Give me a break," Gabriel said.

"Now he's got us going after each other," Andy said. "*Stop* it!"

They stood there looking at each other, Andy between them.

"Sorry," Pik said.

"It's all right," Gabriel said.

"Gentlemen?" Coach asked. "Have you decided practice is over?"

The three of them looked at one another and shook their heads. It was almost funny, really. "Not by a long shot, Coach," Pik called.

"Let's run some plays, Coach," Gabriel called, in his most *helpful young man* voice. They waved to Andy and ran back out onto the field.

Andy almost laughed, watching them go. Then

he realized he couldn't watch any more, so he got up and hobbled off the field, hearing their voices and the sounds of their collisions diminish behind him, until he was far enough from the field that he couldn't hear them at all.

7.
Gabriel

They were all sitting around Thursday night, seven o'clock or so, on a little rise under a tree, watching a PeeWee football game. Why they were watching a PeeWee game they didn't know. Gabriel could tell Andy was still worried about his knee, Pik was still aggravated about the whole situation with the offensive line, and Ray, well, Ray was probably just wondering what he was doing there at all.

Gabriel had rounded up the first two — Pik, who got antsy watching instead of playing football, and Andy, who'd been nursing his knee and brooding in his room when he was supposed to be doing his homework — and had talked them into it. None of them had played PeeWee ball, and the whole idea of kids playing at that age seemed a little silly. Gabriel had said, "It'll be funny to watch these little kids run around crashing into each other. And besides, what else are you guys doing?"

"Well, that's true," Pik had said, hauling himself off his bed.

Andy had taken a little while longer, and Gabriel and Pik had worked on him together. They convinced Andy to join them and led him out to the driveway, Andy looking down at his knee every few steps. Gabriel felt bad for him, but didn't know what else he could do besides getting him out and giving him a chance to think about something else: just letting him know that they were there. On the way to the field on their bikes, Gabriel noticed the way Andy rode, and how he favored his leg.

A few blocks from the field, they'd passed Ray walking the other way. Gabriel decided to make Ray a last-minute addition to the group. Standing on his pedals and coasting, he cut in front of Ray with a stylish skid and asked him to join them. Ray was persuaded to go along by the same logic that worked on Pik: What else was there to do?

So there the four of them were, watching this bogus game. And they were pretty much it, in terms of the crowd. There was an older woman sitting on a lawn chair in the distance, and there were a few parents along the sidelines behind the players, talking to each other. Every now and then a dad would tell his kid to stop crying, get back in there, to keep his chin strap on.

Some kids were still wrestling with their equipment. One kid was experimenting with his shoulder pads on backward. Another kid's helmet — if it *was* his helmet — was so big, it spun on his head. Kids that were already dressed were running into each other in ways that made Gabriel think they were blindfolded. He guessed that they'd seen older players hitting one another before a game to settle their pads, but had no idea why they were doing it.

It looked like chaos out there, the adults trying to round everybody up. The game hadn't started yet, and two kids were crying. One had a bloody nose, and was using the tail of his jersey to stop the bleeding.

"Look at this," Pik said. The kid's mother, a pretty blonde woman, was kneeling before him, shushing him, patting his nose with a Kleenex. The kid kept grabbing for his jersey and his mother kept taking it out of his hands and dabbing his nose with the Kleenex. The kid was wailing. Pik said, "The game hasn't *started* yet."

"Wait'll it *gets* started," Gabriel said.

Nobody in the group seemed to be having a good time. It was funny, but it was also kind of pathetic.

Riding over to get Pik and Andy, Gabriel had felt responsible for their fun, as if he were the host. So he'd stopped off at the 7-Eleven and picked up some candy. Now he handed it out. Pik passed on the Rollos but went for the Starbursts.

Andy passed on both but took a few Tropical Life-savers. Ray took two of everything. Pik watched him, to see if he was going to put it all in his mouth at once. He did. Andy puffed out his cheeks. Gabriel made snorting pig noises.

Finally, both coaches got the kids organized enough to form the lines for the kickoff. The teams were called the Bears and the Raiders. Apparently the coaches hadn't gotten their act together either, because both teams were wearing black. One of the Bears got down in his half stance and his helmet fell over his eyes. A Raider who was back to receive the kick wandered around while he waited. The coaches kept shooing kids off the field who'd then run back on. The referee, who Gabriel recognized as a local plumber, had his whistle in his mouth but kept having to recount the numbers on the field. It took him forever, because everybody was wearing black. Even the helmets didn't help: The Bears' helmets were white, with a little black C on the side, and the Raiders' were all white.

The Bears kicked off. The ball never got more than a foot or so above the ground. It ricocheted off a couple of kids, and there was a lot of panicked running back and forth while both teams kicked it around and chased it. A kid would fall down and the next three kids behind him would fall over him. The ball was finally recovered — or at least

95

a pile of kids formed — out of bounds.

This was sad. This was pathetic. Watching this was bothering all of them. Nobody was talking. Gabriel tried to think of something to say, but couldn't. It was awkward with Ray, the man of silence, there. But considering Pik and Andy's mood, there wouldn't've been all that much chatter anyway. Still, Gabriel wanted to say something; he felt responsible for the lack of fun.

On the field, the referee had finally separated all the kids on the pile. Two were holding onto the ball together and wouldn't let go. It looked like they were on the same team.

Gabriel cleared his throat and looked at Ray, who was gazing out over the field like he'd come in on the middle of the movie. The referee, exasperated, indicated that the Bears would kick again. Pik snorted, and shook his head. After that, the only sound any of them made while the teams were getting set for the kickoff was the occasional smacking sound of Andy sucking on the Lifesavers.

"How's the knee?" Ray finally said. Gabriel looked over at him, but Ray was gazing out at the field.

"Bad," Andy replied. "I'm staying off it."

The Bears kicked off again. The ball bounced off the face guard of the closest Raider, and ricocheted back over the oncoming Bears, where another Raider recovered it deep in Bear territory. The Bears threw their arms up in the air in despair at their luck.

"You gonna be able to play?" Ray asked. Gabriel cringed. *Now* he talks? he thought. And he asks *that*? Though he admitted to himself that it was a question *he'd* wanted to ask, too.

"I don't know," Andy said. He was uncomfortable talking about it, but you could see he wanted to talk to *some*body about it.

"Is it as bad as it was at practice?" Pik asked.

"No, it's not that bad anymore," Andy answered.

" 'Cuz if it was *that* bad . . ." Pik said.

"No, it's not," Andy repeated. Gabriel wondered whether Andy was covering up how bad it really was.

The Raiders ran a sweep, something like USC's Student Body Left, but at this level it resembled something more like recess getting out. Both teams milled around for ten yards and fell in a heap.

"You could start out just on offense," Pik said, "while you test it out. On offense it'd be easier to go at your own speed, not do anything you didn't think you could do."

"That's a good idea," Gabriel said.

"I'm full of good ideas," Pik replied.

The quarterback of the Raiders went back to

pass, took advantage of the general confusion, and ran out of the pocket for fifteen yards before he fell over for no reason Gabriel could see. Andy, watching the action, put a hand out in Gabriel's direction and Gabriel filled it with two more Lifesavers.

"Speaking of good ideas," Andy said. "What'd you say to Duggan that time?"

They watched the little kids run into each other. Gabriel thought to himself: *What is it about this game that's making me so sad?*

"Ray?" Andy said. "Hello?"

"*What* time?" Ray asked.

"You know," Andy said. "*That* time."

"I know," Pik said. "What'd you say? The guy looked totally freaked."

The Raider quarterback tried the same play, the quarterback sneak, and it worked again, except that the ball, too big for his hands, squirted out as he headed for the goal line, and rolled through the back of the end zone.

"I told him I would go home and get a hammer and come back and beat him to death with it," Ray told them.

"You're kidding," Pik said.

"No," Ray said. "And a few days later, a couple of those guys came by the house, and I showed them the hammer."

The referee was signalling Bears' ball, and the

Raiders were jumping around in anguish and yelling at their quarterback.

"You went after them with a hammer?" Andy asked. He was sitting up.

"No," Ray said. "They came by the house, so I showed it to them."

"What'd they say?" Pik said, incredulous.

"They thought it was a good hammer," Ray answered. "Then they remembered they had to be someplace else." He was watching the game. The Bears tried throwing a pass. The quarterback threw it as high as he could. It traveled seven or eight yards downfield. Four players from both teams settled under it, and no one caught it.

Gabriel stared at Ray. He didn't believe Ray would hit anyone with a hammer, though he didn't know him that well. And Ray sure must've convinced Duggan.

"You're nuts," Andy said.

"That's what they said," Ray answered. "They said, 'You're nuts.'"

"*I* think you are," Andy replied. "What'd you say?"

"I said, 'Here's my hammer,'" Ray said. He smiled.

"*Terminator 2*," Gabriel said.

"That's right," Ray added. "It's like Arnold says, after he shoots the guys in the knees: 'They'll live.'"

"Give me a break," Pik said. "You don't go around threatening guys with hammers."

"He wouldn't hit anyone with a hammer," Gabriel said.

"They left people alone after that," Ray said. "Didn't they?"

"I don't believe this," Andy said. "Suppose they told Coach."

Ray looked at him. "Now what does Coach ever do about anything?" he asked.

"He's got a point *there*," Andy said.

"Suppose they called the cops," Pik said.

"Yeah," Ray said. "Duggan's really gonna do that."

Andy laughed. He did an exaggeratedly whiney voice: " 'Hello, officer? My friend on the team says he's gonna *hit* me with a *hammer*.' "

Gabriel looked at him a while longer, and then shook his head and returned his attention to the PeeWees. "Oh, boy," he said.

The Bears had somehow mounted a drive and were threatening to score. They lined up for a field goal, which Gabriel figured had to be a fake. No way this crew ever got organized enough to get off a successful field goal. And sure enough it *was* a fake, and it fooled the Raiders who all ran to the kicker and knocked him down while the holder jogged into the end zone like a little boy carrying his lunch to school. He was mobbed by happy teammates.

"Give me a break," Pik said. "A hammer."

"Coulda been worse," Andy added. "Coulda been his Dad's power saw."

"Yeah, but he woulda had to plug it in," Pik replied.

"That's right. Imagine he's running after them and the plug pulls out," Gabriel said, and they all laughed.

Andy said, "Or he could get a table saw and roll it around after them."

Pik added, "Or you know one of those giant things, what do you call them, *lathes* or something."

"Or a wood chipper," Gabriel said, and they all were wildly grossed out by his suggestion, except not really, and afterward they felt better. They were even less mad at the offensive line, as if just bringing up the wood chipper had made them see again exactly how stupid all of this was.

The Bears got the ball back on a fumble, and a kid who must've gotten there late, and who was a helmet taller than anyone else, was running the ball. He ran over four or five kids as if he were King Fullback, and scored.

"Is that kid the same age as the other kids?" Andy asked.

"That's what I was thinking," Pik said. "He looks like somebody's older brother."

"Or father," Ray said, and they laughed.

But it wasn't funny. On defense, the kid lined up at the end position and threw blockers around like Godzilla in Tokyo and then just decked the poor kid playing quarterback for the Raiders. The Raider quarterback lay there on his back, quiet for a second, and then started wailing. He looked like he'd gotten the wind knocked out of him. He got up and left the field crying and shaking his head.

"Man, I don't like this at all," Pik said. Nobody disagreed with him.

The older woman in the lawn chair, maybe somebody's grandmother, was still sitting a little distance away from them. "Excuse me, ma'am," Andy yelled, getting her attention. When she looked over, he said, "Is that big kid the same age as the other kids?"

"Jamie?" the woman said.

"Number 32," Andy said. "The guy who just scored."

"That's Jamie," the woman said. "Yes, he's their age."

They were uncomfortably silent. " 'Cuz he looks older," Pik added.

"Yes, he does," the woman answered. "But you know the way kids grow at that age."

"Jeez," Andy said. They watched while Jamie, the big kid, sacked the Raiders' second-string quarterback, who was so frightened he fumbled. Jamie recovered. On the Bears' first offensive play, Jamie took the ball up the middle and scored, trampling a Raider or two on the way. More kids were crying.

"Talk about your mismatches," Gabriel said.

"They shouldn't let kids like that play," Andy said.

"What're you gonna do?" Pik asked. "Tell him he can't play because he's too good?"

"In that case, yeah," Andy said.

"They should do that with us, then," Gabriel said, and as soon as he said it, he realized it hadn't gone over the way he thought it would. They were all looking out at the field and thinking about the number of people *they'd* hammered, even at the junior-high level. What was so different about this? Hadn't they also come along faster than some of the kids they played with?

"Let's get outta here," Pik said. "I don't want to watch anymore of this."

"Neither do I," Andy added.

"Sorry," Gabriel said. They got up and got on their bikes. Ray climbed on Gabriel's handlebars, the way he had for the ride down here. "I thought this'd be fun."

"Yeah, well," Pik said.

"Let's go," Andy said.

"All right, all right," Gabriel said. As he started to pedal, starting off slowly because of Ray's weight up front, he said, "Let's go over Ray's and see the hammer."

"The table saw," Pik said.

"The wood chipper," Andy said. All together they made that *we're grossed out* sound, and kept making it as they pedalled up the hill. Gabriel was still wobbling but was starting to keep up. Ray was enjoying the ride and leaning back for support, bumping Gabriel's shoulder with every turn of the pedals.

8.
The Team

In the middle of the week before the Flood game it turned cold, and an icy rain came down out of a dismal gray sky. Later, Gabriel would remember what a long week it was, how dark it would get by the time practice ended, how the cold, wind-blown October rain felt like needles on his face and hands, how miserable and long those practices became.

But by Friday evening, the sky had cleared and the weather had turned nice. The condition of the Flood playing field was nearly perfect: The ground was wet but not sodden, and traction was good. There was no wind. On this night, the players, not the weather, would decide the outcome of the game.

In the locker room just before the opening kick-off, Coach Kohut sat the team down for a few final words. They were dressed in their maroon jerseys and gold pants, warmed up, ready to go.

"This game is important," Coach told them, "because Flood's record is the same as ours, no losses. Both teams figure to win their two remaining games. So whoever wins tonight will almost certainly win the League Championship."

Looking around at his teammates — taped up, sweating, some of their maroon jerseys and gold pants already grass-stained from the warm-ups — looking around the locker room, Gabriel felt nervous. The whole season rested on this game. There was a large crowd out there, including his parents. He didn't know if the line would play to win, or try to hurt him by letting guys through. And worst of all, Flood had a player who could put him in the hospital.

At the first practice of the week, Coach had told them about the Flood defensive end who was bigger by twenty or thirty pounds than anybody on Johnson, including Charlie Izzo. He told them this kid had been destroying linemen and backs all season. All week they'd been practicing running right, away from Flood's right defensive end, number 17.

"The Hammer," Andy said.

"The Chainsaw," Pik said.

"The Wood Chipper," Ray added.

"Chip," Gabriel decided. "Let's call him Chip."

"You fellas have something to contribute to this conversation?" Coach had asked, looking their way. It was not really a conversation, it was a speech. Coach was giving it before practice began, Monday afternoon. Everyone was sitting around the end zone. They'd warmed up, and then Coach Kohut had sat them down before the real work began.

"Let's call him Chip," Gabriel repeated. "We need to, uh, *demythologize* him." Gabriel drew the word out.

"De-what?" Coach said.

A few of the players laughed.

Gabriel started to explain. "See, I found this word in the dictionary," he said. "It means — "

"I know what it means," Coach said. "It means it'll bring him down a notch or two in your mind, make him less of a big deal. But let me tell you something. This kid *is* a big deal. He'll clean your clock, and then he'll ask you what time it is. And if you don't know, he'll clean it for you all over again. He's already put two kids in the hospital."

That got their attention.

The name Chip stuck and, all week long, Coach worked the team hard, practicing plays that kept the flow away from Chip. He worked with Gabriel on getting rid of the ball quickly. He put two scrubeenies opposite Ronnie Duggan, calling them "Chip and Chop," and told Ronnie to keep both of them out of the backfield. He had the backs — second stringers as well as starters — practice running to the right side, away from Chip.

They got the picture: Coach's strategy was to do everything he could to avoid Chip.

All that week during practice, Andy paced the sidelines in despair. On Monday, as Ray had suggested, he tried a couple of running plays on offense, tentatively, testing the knee. After three carries he gave up. "I can't cut," he told Coach. "It feels funny."

"I'll put Picarazzi in there," Coach told him. He thought it over for a moment, then asked, "Can you kick?"

"I don't think so," Andy replied.

"Punt? Field goals?"

"It's my kicking leg, and it hurts when I — "

"All right," Coach said. "I'll have Picarazzi practice kicking, too. What did the doctor say?"

"Excuse me?"

"You've seen a doctor, haven't you?"

"Uh, I have an appointment." Andy felt ashamed for saying that, because it wasn't true.

"All right," Coach said. "Let me know what you find out."

But when Gabriel asked him about it later in the week, Andy said he wanted to wait a few days, maybe it would get better by itself, maybe it would feel better by Friday. He continued to dress for practice and warm up with the team; he just didn't scrimmage. "I'm gonna contribute," he told Gabriel. "I swear it. I'm gonna suit up on Friday, and somehow I'm gonna help us beat Flood."

To make matters worse, Andy's father said something during the week about coming to the game. "I may be able to get there," he told Andy. "If I can get away from the hospital early that evening, I'll go straight to the game."

What if he sees I'm not playing? Andy thought. He felt guilty, now, for not having mentioned the knee to his father right after he injured it. So he said nothing.

Pik ran the drills and scrimmages that week at three-quarter speed. His ankle was sore, he told Gabriel. Every day after practice he would hurry home and ice it down.

At school on Friday, Gabriel realized that Pik was still limping. He asked him about it.

"Still sore," Pik told him. "But I'll be a hundred percent tonight, no question. I gotta be. We gotta beat Flood."

That night, in the locker room before the game, Coach Kohut reminded them they'd be up against the toughest opponent they'd face all season. He went over a couple of key plays once more, then reminded them how important the game was.

"But don't think about winning or losing," he told them. "Not at first. Just play hard, one play at a time. Remember your assignments. Stay intense out there, concentrate. Hit somebody. Hit somebody hard. . . . Okay, let's go play some football."

On the field, under the lights, Gabriel and Tony Picarazzi dropped back near the ten-yard line to receive the opening kick. Looking downfield, Gabriel saw a line of white: the Flood eleven, wearing white pants, white jerseys, white helmets.

Who do they think they are, he thought, the good guys?

Chip was easy to pick out: He was a full helmet taller than any kid on his team, and the only player whose sleeves were cut off above the elbow. He had tucked the cut-off sleeves up under his shoulder pads so that his upper arms were fully visible. They were enormous.

"You see him?" Tony Picarazzi yelled over to Gabriel. "What's he do, eat hormones for breakfast?"

"And steroids for lunch," Gabriel said. "He's a pharmacy."

The referee behind them blew his whistle and the Flood kicker ran at the ball. The ball went up into the lights and floated down and, as Gabriel caught it, he heard Tony yell "Right!" and he took off behind him, his eyes scanning the melee in front of him. He was glad to see Chip's tall figure way off to the left. He saw Tony cut down a hard-charging white jersey, and then he accelerated through a gap near the right sideline and turned on the afterburners. That was when something very large and very solid hit him like a freight train and sent him flying. When he hit the ground, the impact knocked the ball out of his hands.

Fortunately, he'd been knocked clear out of bounds. He got up quickly, feeling exhilarated — it had been a good, clean hit. He looked around and there was Chip, just starting to get up. "Nice tackle," Gabriel said, and he meant it. He offered his hand.

Chip reached out and pulled himself to his feet, a long pull. His grinning face stared down at Gabriel: freckles, a flat nose, and a mouth guard hanging from his face mask, a shiny string of saliva dangling from it. "You're a landmark, kid," Chip said, squeezing Gabriel's hand, hard. "I'm gonna bury you."

"Not on your best day, pal," Gabriel replied. A little Chuck Norris tough-guy talk for the big guy. He squeezed back just as hard. Then he pulled his hand away and trotted out toward the huddle.

But that opening play set the stage for things to come. Johnson's running game went no-where — Chip could cover an amazing amount of ground. Gradually the truth dawned on Gabriel: Running away from him wasn't working. Chip

wasn't real fast, but he was fast enough, and he
had an instinct — he always seemed to wind up
around the ball. He would take the proper pursuit
angle and cut off the run, making tackles up and
down the line of scrimmage — brutal tackles,
coming in from the side and slamming into Tony
or Ray, hitting them low and hard and driving
into them with his shoulder, pounding them into
the turf. Like he'd said: burying them. It didn't
matter whether or not Duggan and Izzo and those
guys were trying hard to block: Chip was destroying everything. It was hit, crunch, and burn.

Neither Ray nor Tony could juke him or outrun
him. If Duggan or Marcus or a tight end managed
to block him, he didn't stay blocked: Somehow he
would get up and reach out an arm to bring down
the ball carrier.

When Gabriel tried to pass, it always seemed
to be second and long or third and long. He'd hold
the ball while the receivers ran their patterns,
then get clobbered before or just as he released
the ball.

On defense, though, Johnson was holding its
own. Chip wasn't as much a factor on offense: he
played right tackle — ferociously — but there
was no way he could block Duggan *and* Pik *and*
Ray *and* Gabriel. Ray stopped up the middle, Pik
jammed the sweeps and off-tackle plays to the left,

and Gabriel shut down everything that got past the linebackers. Johnson's swarming defense kept forcing Flood to punt the ball.

By well into the second quarter, nobody had scored. The game was turning into a low-scoring duel, like a boxing match with both fighters slugging it out: The game would go to the fighter still punching in the late rounds, the fourth quarter.

Despite Chip, it was Johnson that landed the first big blow. Midway through the second quarter, when Flood lined up to punt from their own forty-five, Ray slipped between two linemen, crashed through a blocking halfback and dove toward the punter. The ball ricocheted off his arm and bounced all the way back to the fifteen, where it was covered by a swarm of elated guys in maroon. From there, Gabriel tried a short pass (deflected), an off-tackle play to the right side (stopped by Chip, gain of two), and a student-body right (tackle by Chip and someone else, gain of half a yard).

As the field-goal unit was coming onto the field, Gabriel looked over at the bench. Andy was sitting there with his head down. He looked like he was trying to hide.

They lined up. Gabriel knelt, ready to take the snap from Izzo. He looked up at Picarazzi. "Ready?"

Tony looked nervous. He wiped his hands on his thighs, then looked up toward the goalpost.

He looked back down at Gabriel, and nodded.

If you miss this, Gabriel thought. . . .

He called the signals, got a good snap from Izzo and set it up well —

Tony's foot came through, a split-second late, Gabriel thought.

The kick sounded off, somehow: short, maybe, or way wide.

He looked up and saw the ball wobble through the uprights like a wounded duck.

Gabriel leaped up, arms in the air. He pounded Tony on the back.

Johnson had the lead, 3–0.

The score seemed to light a fire under the Flood offense. On their next drive, they mixed flare passes with quick-breaking bursts off tackle and moved the ball steadily downfield. They scored while there were still a few minutes left in the half, held Johnson on their next possession, got the ball back on Picarazzi's punt, and started marching back toward Johnson's goal line. They probed every aspect of the Johnson defense until they found a tender spot at free safety, where Tony Picarazzi was playing deep, way off the receivers cutting across the middle in front of him.

They started completing short passes with ease.

Frustrated, Gabriel shouted over to Tony, "Come up on 'em, play 'em tighter!"

"Can't let 'em get behind me!" Tony yelled back.

Flood kept completing passes in front of Tony, and their quick off-tackle plays picked up four or five yards a pop before Ray or Gabriel could get to the ball carriers. Flood made it into the end zone before the clock ran out.

The half ended with the score a depressing 14–3.

During halftime, Gabriel sat on the locker room floor, holding his helmet and staring at his cleats. He was tired and disgusted. He didn't see how they could come back and win. Chip was a monster — they'd never score on that guy! And he missed Andy on defense. Try talking to Tony! You couldn't say a thing to that guy. Flood would be throwing short passes in front of him all night.

Coach Kohut talked about first-half mistakes and went over adjustments for the second half. Gabriel soon realized that Coach had no new ideas: The adjustments were small ones, insignificant. The second half was going to be more of the same.

But Gabriel didn't have any better ideas, so he kept his mouth shut.

Andy was sitting next to him, his uniform sparkling clean, looking despondent. He nudged Gabriel. "We ought to be running *at* Chip," he said quietly, so Coach wouldn't hear.

"What are you, crazy?" Gabriel said.

"Nothing else is working."

"Hey," Gabriel asked, "did your dad show up yet?"

"Yeah, late in the half," Andy replied. "I pretended I didn't see him. But I'm pretty sure he saw me sitting on the bench."

"He's gonna ask you why, right?"

Andy nodded, and sighed. He looked crushed. "I've been wanting him to come to a game for so long, to see me play. And now this. I can't believe it."

Pik and Ray, sitting on the floor on Gabriel's other side, looked tired and beat-up. Pik's jersey had two ragged holes in it, and the cut on the bridge of his nose had opened up and bled all over one side of his face. Ray's jersey had its numerals, both front and back, completely obliterated by mud and line-chalk.

Over by the chalkboard, Coach was launching into the inspirational closing segment of his halftime speech: "I don't know what you call what you're playing out there," he was saying, "but it isn't football. You're going to have to play with a lot more concentration, a lot more intensity, if you expect to beat this team. They've got good players and they're well coached and in good physical condition. And, of course, Chip is having his usual NFL-level day. So if you want to beat Flood, you're going to have to dig deep down and come up with the guts and the courage to go all out for thirty more minutes. I know you can beat them, but it's up to you. You have to *want* to win. More than they do. So let me hear you. Do you want it?"

"Yes," they yelled.

"I can't hear you. Do you want this game?"

"Yes!"

"Want it bad?"

"YES!"

"You gonna win?"

"*YES!*"

"What are you waiting for then?"

As Gabriel filed out of the locker room with the rest of the team, he realized to his surprise that a few of Coach's words were still echoing in his head. I know you can beat them, but it's up to you. I know you can beat them, but it's up to you. I know you can beat them, *but it's up to you.*

It's up to me, Gabriel thought. Then he thought, No, it's up to all of us. That's who it's up to, the team.

He started thinking.

What sort of adjustments could they make that Coach hadn't thought of?

How do you beat a guy like Chip?

What do you do when everything you've practiced hard, all week long, fails to work?

Gabriel picked up a ball and found Pik. They stood on the sidelines and tossed the ball back and forth, waiting for the start of the second half. Gabriel thought things over.

Tony Picarazzi wandered by and stood beside him, catching every other ball Pik threw.

Gabriel said, "Tony, listen, on defense, you have to come up some, play tighter. We got to cut off that short pass."

Tony gave him a look. "I told you, I don't want to let anybody get behind me. I'm the last line of defense out there."

Gabriel thought: He's a co-captain. He'll never do anything I suggest. I've got to get *him* to come up with it.

"What do you think of their quarterback?" he said.

Tony caught the ball and winged it back to Pik. "He's pretty good. He floats it right in there."

It has to be like fishing, Gabriel was thinking. You don't go out and hook the fish; the fish has to come to the bait.

"The guy's good," Gabriel said, "throwing short passes. He's got a nice soft touch."

"Very accurate."

Gabriel asked, "Wonder why he hasn't thrown

118

it deep yet." Throwing the bait out there.

"I'm playing 'em deep."

"But they haven't even run deep patterns." Wiggling the bait around.

Tony thought it over. "That's true," he said. "The receivers don't even fake it deep."

It was a nibble. Gabriel tried to set the hook. "Maybe they don't have deep patterns in their play book."

"Why wouldn't they?" Tony asked.

"Beats me," Gabriel said.

"Noodle-arm!" Tony said excitedly.

Big strike. Big fish.

Tony said, "You know, he hasn't thrown a pass with any mustard on it. Those short little passes just float in there. I'll bet the guy couldn't throw deep on a bet."

"That makes sense," Gabriel said. "You're probably right."

Tony trotted off. Gabriel continued to throw to Pik and mull things over.

A moment later, Andy hobbled up to him.

"What's happening?" Gabriel asked.

"I wish the half would start," Andy replied. "I'm wearing myself out, ducking my dad."

Gabriel chuckled, then said, "So, what'd you notice from the sidelines in the first half? Any ideas?"

"The corner's playing right up on Pik," Andy

said. "They know you've gotta get rid of the ball. The strong safety's been coming up fast, too. You could hit Pik, long."

"If I could get the time."

"Right."

"Chip's a chain saw out there," Gabriel said. "Ronnie couldn't keep him out of the backfield with a twelve-gauge. Uh-oh," he said, "here comes your dad."

"Oh, man."

Dr. Kim called out, "Andy!" It was sort of a command. He was walking toward them, his overcoat open and his tie streaming over his shoulder.

"Later," Andy said, and headed off to meet his father.

Pik came over and said, "Andy thinks I could get open deep?"

"Yeah."

"This is not news to me. I know I could. My ankle's better — I've got speed out there. If you could get some decent protection. . . ."

"I'll keep it in mind." Gabriel backed away from Pik and tossed him the football. "Let me throw some more."

He threw a couple of bullets that hit Pik in the numbers. Then he looked around for Andy. He and his father were standing near the bench, sort of turned away from each other, looking at the ground. Andy was doing the talking.

Ray came up to Gabriel and stood beside him.

" 'S up?" Gabriel asked.

"We gotta do something," Ray said. "We can beat this buncha preppies."

"I know it."

"We just ain't calling the right plays."

Gabriel chuckled. "What do you mean 'we,' *pal?*"

Ray grinned. "*Coach* ain't calling the right plays."

"You want to call different plays?"

"*Some*body better," said Ray.

Gabriel asked, "You know what'll happen if I try to change the call, with those older guys in the huddle?"

Ray nodded, and spat. "All I can say is, I'm sick and tired of having that big sucker hitting me from the side, tripping me up from behind. I'd like to get in his face, go straight at him for a change. Knock him down a few times. Wood chipper my butt." Ray spat again and walked away.

Gabriel flicked the ball to Pik.

Maybe Andy was right, back in the locker room, he thought — maybe we ought to try running *at* the guy.

He glanced toward the bench and was surprised to see Andy sitting down, one pant leg rolled way up, his father kneeling on the ground before him. He was holding Andy's calf with one hand, his thigh with the other, and he was moving the leg first from side to side, then up and down. A moment later, when Gabriel looked back again, Dr. Kim had a roll of tape in his hand. He must've gotten it from the trainer. As Gabriel watched, Andy's father began gently to tape Andy's knee and leg. His hands looked like they knew what they were doing.

Early in the third quarter, Gabriel again tried to pass on third and long, but Chip flattened Ronnie Duggan, crashed through and sacked Gabe.

Lying on the ground beneath the big kid, Gabriel heard Chip say, "You're gonna be eating grass the whole second half, punk."

"Moo," said Gabriel. He shoved Chip off him and stood up. "Moooo-oooo." He said it loud, and players on both teams turned their heads.

"Hey, wise guy," Chip said. "Where'd number 38 learn to block, ballet class? Tell him I said that."

"And I'm telling *you*, break it up," said one of the referees.

Gabriel walked away. In the huddle, he said: "Hey, Ronnie, Chip says you must've learned to block in ballet class."

Ronnie wiped the sweat off his cheek, leaving a dark red smear. A bloody raspberry, the color of his jersey, ran the length of his forearm.

He shook his head. "That kid is huge."

"Come *on!*" Gabriel insisted. "You can handle him."

"Shut up, Fixx," Charlie Izzo said.

Ronnie looked determined. "He won't be talking ballet at the end of the game, I swear," he said.

A player arrived from the sideline with the next play.

Gabriel realized it wouldn't be enough just to get Ronnie fired up — he'd have to pull the rest of the team into it, too.

They ran the next play, the one Coach had sent in: He faked to Ray going left and handed off to Tony, who followed one of the guards around the right end. Chip slid along the line of scrimmage and tackled Tony as he tried to turn the corner. The play lost a yard.

In the huddle, Gabriel asked, "Any way to get more guys blocking Chip?"

Pik said, "Got a tank?"

"We're double-teaming him half the time already," said Dave Booth.

"The quarterback could block," Duggan said.

"Yeah, that might work," Izzo added, grinning at Gabriel.

"Tony and I could both block," Ray said, "and the quarterback could run it."

"Yeah, you carry the ball, Fixx," Tony said. "It'll give us an extra blocker."

Gabriel ran a keeper to the right. It seemed to

123

him that he was following half of the Johnson Junior High School around the right end: Both Ray and Tony were out in front of him as well as the whole right side of the line. Chip came in like a bowling ball and knocked the blockers into one another, then reached out with one arm and dragged Gabriel down.

But he picked up three yards.

"What was that?" Coach yelled at them from the sidelines. "Who called that play?"

They ran it again. Gabriel cut back and Chip barely caught a piece of his jersey. Gabriel picked up a first down.

Coach dropped his clipboard on the ground and kicked it. "What are you doing?" he shouted. But when he saw the guys moving the down markers, he clapped his hands. "First down! Way to go!"

They ran it a couple more times. The play gained four, then two yards.

"Okay," Ronnie said in the huddle. "They're keying on the quarterback, now's the time to pass."

"Yeah, fake a run, then throw it to Pik," Tony said.

"I'll be open," Pik said. "Run right. I'll find a seam in the middle, near the sideline."

"Use run blocking, none of this backpedalling junk," said Ronnie.

"On three," Gabriel said, and they broke the huddle.

Gabriel felt a surge of excitement. The idea was not to be in charge, but to play as a team. They were beginning to work together.

They moved the ball down the field, improvising, working off what they'd just done, mostly running, and picking up three or four yards a crack. The drive took precious minutes off the clock. They got down near the Flood goal line, but then stalled. On fourth and seven from the nineteen, Coach again sent in the field-goal unit.

But Andy didn't come in. Picarazzi would kick again.

They lined up, Gabriel kneeling to receive the snap from Izzo. He called the signals.

The ball came spiraling back to him.

He set it up perfectly.

Again it seemed that Tony was late getting to the ball. His foot made solid contact.

Thump!

Smack!

Gabriel knew that sound: Somebody had gotten a hand on the ball.

He looked up. The kick missed wide by a yard, and the guys in white jerseys celebrated.

The score stood at 14–3, and the third quarter was gone.

They got the ball back on a punt deep in their own territory with barely ten minutes showing on the clock. Coach sent in a running play — same old stuff, an off-tackle slant to the right.

In the huddle, somebody suggested a pass. Gabriel called for a short pass to the right. He took the snap from Izzo, backpedalled, and out of the corner of his eye saw Chip flatten Ronnie Duggan and head straight for him. He scrambled left, trying to get around Chip, when Ronnie got up and cut Chip's legs out from under him. The big guy dropped like a dead quail.

Gabriel headed upfield. They ran him out of bounds seventeen yards later.

On the way back to the huddle, Gabriel exchanged high-fives and low-fives with Pik and Ray.

But the mood changed in the huddle.

"That was supposed to be a *pass*, Fixx," said Dave Booth.

"Hogging it," Charlie Izzo said. "Showboating."

Lenny Marcus asked, "Hey Fixx, you think you can win it by yourself?"

"Guys, shut up," Ray said. "That was our longest gain of the day."

"Nice block, Ronnie," Tony said.

126

"Oh," said Pik, "did Duggan finally block somebody?"

"Shut up, Pik," Gabriel said. But it was too late.

Charlie Izzo said, "Come on, Ronnie, let's stop blocking for these punks."

There was a stunned silence. Nobody could believe he'd said it out loud.

Ray stood up and caught the eye of an official. He made a "T" with his hands. The ref called time out.

From the sideline, Coach hollered: "What's going on out there!"

A kid jogged onto the field with water bottles.

Ray asked, "When are you gonna quit bickering? When are you gonna wake up and play for yourselves? You ain't playing for each other. Duggan ain't playing for Fixx, and Izzo ain't playing for Telander. Duggan's playing for Duggan, Izzo for Izzo. After all you been through, you want to hand it to Flood? Where's your pride?"

"You're wrong," Duggan said. "I'm not playing for myself. It may not have occurred to you, DeVellis, but I'm not enjoying having Big Chip smash my face in. If it was just for me, I wouldn't stick around here for one more minute. I'd walk away. I'm playing for Johnson. Izzo, you better keep blocking. You volunteered to play for Johnson, nobody made you. Just because there're some little geeks and wimps on this team who don't know their place, that doesn't mean they can't play football. They can. They are. And besides, do you want some preppie saying you stink because Flood kicked our butts tonight? If I see Chip shopping at Brooks Brothers on Christmas Eve, I want to tell him *we* kicked his butt, not me, not you, DeVellis, not you, Charlie, but *us*. Johnson."

Somebody blew a whistle. The water boy started collecting bottles.

Charlie Izzo said, "Call a play, Fixx."

Two plays later, third-and-six, as they were huddling up, Andy raced out onto the field and tapped Picarazzi on the shoulder. Tony hesitated, then broke away and headed toward the bench.

Gabriel asked Andy about his knee.

"My dad says it's not injured bad. This tape job's amazing, it feels okay. Maybe I can outrun Big Chip."

"Cow chip," said Charlie Izzo.

"Mooooooo!" said Lenny Marcus.

Everybody laughed.

They're loose, Gabriel thought. And together. "Nothing's been working," he said to Andy. "We're tried everything."

"You're wrong," Duggan said. "You haven't called my number all day."

"What do you mean?" Gabriel asked, knowing full well what he meant.

"I mean, stupid, we haven't run over left tackle."

"Try that quarterback keeper again," Ray said, "except this time we're not gonna run *away* from the guy, we're gonna run *at* him."

"Everybody block."

"I like that," Ronnie said. "I'm gonna block straight ahead. Fixx, make a cut in whichever way he doesn't go."

"Let Kim run it," Marcus added. "His legs are fresh."

"Student body over left tackle," Gabriel said. "Andy carries. On one."

Duggan fired out at Chip, and Ray nearly knocked him off his feet. Andy found a little hole and sped through it, but Chip reached out and grabbed his leg. Andy went down hard.

Gabriel held his breath. But Andy got right up and walked toward the huddle without a limp.

It was fourth-and-two.

"Good block, DeVellis," Marcus said.

"The Hammer," Booth said.

The linemen snickered.

"Hammer that guy good, DeVellis," Ronnie Duggan said. "I'll nail him, you hammer him."

"You got it, Duggan," Ray said.

Roofing nails, Gabriel thought. Galvanized roofing nails.

Gabriel liked words — all kinds of words —

and sometimes he read the dictionary for fun, just flipped it open at a random page and started reading, finding words that meant things he'd been wondering about. Now a word popped into his head, one he'd read about but didn't have anything to apply it to, until now. *Galvanized.* That's what was happening here: The team had been shocked into action by a superior player on the other team. Big Chip had galvanized them.

Gabriel's mind snapped back to the game.

The huddle. Ten guys staring at him.

What am I *thinking?*

Picarazzi was standing there. "Coach says to punt."

Gabriel said, "Tony, we gotta go for it. There're only six minutes left."

"What play?" Tony asked.

Duggan said: "Student body over left tackle."

Gabriel said: "On two."

Tony sped off the field as the team broke the huddle and took up positions at the line of scrimmage.

"That's the wrong formation!" the Coach hollered.

Gabriel ignored him. He looked over the defense. The safeties had moved forward a foot or two. The linebackers were also pressing in closer to the line of scrimmage. To his left, Chip was breathing hard.

"It's fourth down!" yelled the Coach.

"Ready!" yelled Gabriel.

The Johnson line went half-way down, elbows on their knees.

"Set!"

The line hunched down into their three-point stances.

"Hut-one! Hut-two!"

Motion exploded all around him. The ball was slapped into his palms and he spun and took two steps, letting Ray slide past. He stuffed the ball in Andy's gut and carried out the fake bootleg, looking back over his shoulder as the play developed.

Ronnie hit Chip low and stood him up.

Ray knocked him off his feet.

When he started to get up, Ronnie fell on him.

They buried Chip. They planted him like a shrub.

Andy flashed through the hole past Chip, juked a linebacker and headed down the sideline. He was finally dragged down by two players twelve yards downfield.

Chip got up slowly.

By the time they scored their first touchdown, two more minutes had ticked off the clock.

Andy's kick for the extra point was perfect. It was 14–10. A field goal would do no good; they needed another touchdown. And they had only four minutes left.

Flood ran Andy's kickoff back to their own thirty-two. Throughout the third and most of the fourth quarter, Flood had played conservatively, sticking to the run to protect the ball, but now they opened up their attack once again, mixing short passes with running plays. They started a well-balanced drive upfield, staying inbounds, chewing up turf and the clock at the same time.

Picarazzi had stayed in for Andy at free safety, only now he was covering guys tighter. He knocked one pass down, and a couple of plays later he clobbered a receiver just as the ball got there, and the guy dropped it.

It created a third-and-long situation. After taking a time out, Flood tried a long pass over on Tony's side of the field. The receiver juked Tony and sped past him. Gabriel raced over to help out, but he had no chance.

It didn't matter: The ball was underthrown. Tony circled beneath it and picked it off. He ran it back to the Johnson thirty.

Time was running out. They had less than a minute to score.

Johnson ran a couple plays. They ignored the plays Coach sent in, calling their own, but Coach didn't seem to mind. He kept sending in plays anyway, going through the motions, but he wasn't hollering at them any longer. He seemed to have turned the game over to them. It was theirs to win or lose.

With eighteen seconds left on the scoreboard, they called their last time out. They'd only gotten to their own forty-five.

"The *clock*, Fixx — we need a long pass," Duggan said.

"I can't pass it deep, Ronnie. I'm not getting time. Chip's been getting in all night."

"We gotta give him time!"

"We gotta block Chip!"

The line was into it, Gabriel could see. They'd paid the price, though, and the cost had been high. One side of Marcus's face looked like chopped meat — hamburger, or maybe cat food. Booth's hand was bandaged (when had that happened? Gabriel wondered), and Freed had blood all over his gold pants, either his own blood or that of Flood's tackle.

"Try passing off a fake running play," Duggan said. "We can use run blocking to give you time."

"Yeah," Ray said, "fake the run and roll out."

"We'll take care of Chip," Duggan said. "Throw it to Telander, deep."

"Okay," Gabriel said. He loved it — everybody was contributing. "Student body left, I'll roll right and hit Telander deep along the right sideline. On two."

"Don't drop it," Charlie Izzo said to Pik as they broke the huddle. "Don't you drop it."

Pik said nothing. He lined up wide to the right and looked over the secondary. With only seconds left in the game, the cornerback was giving him more of a cushion. The strong safety had backed off, too. The crowd was screaming in his ear and he couldn't hear Gabriel calling signals, so he watched the ball out of the corner of his eye. When Izzo snapped it, he took off at three-quarter speed. He ran right at the cornerback, watching his eyes all the way. . . . The guy backpedalled, looking in toward the action around the quarterback . . . and then he went for the fake run, cutting back toward the line of scrimmage, glancing at Pik, expecting Pik to block him.

The safety went for the run, too, taking a few precious steps forward, and Pik suddenly found himself behind the coverage, running free and clear down the sideline, running at full speed, running . . .

He looked back over his shoulder.

If only Gabriel could get enough time to set up . . .

134

And then he saw the ball. It left the mass of bodies back at the line of scrimmage and climbed toward the black night sky, gaining altitude. . . .

The ball hung there. . . .

Gabriel sure can launch 'em, Pik thought.

He turned up the speed a notch. His ankle felt fine.

Then he was running under the ball as it came down, down . . .

He felt it settle into his hands and he tucked it in. It felt good, as if it belonged there.

Behind him, the Flood free safety made a last desperate lunge for his ankles. He hit the ground hard, his fingers clawing at Pik's heels.

Pik raced into the end zone, untouched.

The stadium clock showed 00:03. Kicking the extra point would use up the final three seconds. Johnson had won.

Pik, remembering the PeeWee game, went back and gave the Flood safety a hand up.

Through his face mask, the kid looked surprised. "Thanks," he said.

"Don't mention it," Pik replied. "You guys played a heck of a game."

"So did you," the kid said. "All you guys did. The whole team."

"That's the idea," Pik said. He grinned. He felt better than he'd felt in a long time.

Then his teammates mobbed him. All of them.

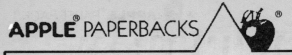

APPLE® PAPERBACKS

Pick an Apple and Polish Off Some Great Reading!

BEST-SELLING APPLE TITLES

❏ MT43944-8	**Afternoon of the Elves** Janet Taylor Lisle	$2.75
❏ MT43109-9	**Boys Are Yucko** Anna Grossnickle Hines	$2.75
❏ MT43473-X	**The Broccoli Tapes** Jan Slepian	$2.95
❏ MT42709-1	**Christina's Ghost** Betty Ren Wright	$2.75
❏ MT43461-6	**The Dollhouse Murders** Betty Ren Wright	$2.75
❏ MT43444-6	**Ghosts Beneath Our Feet** Betty Ren Wright	$2.75
❏ MT44351-8	**Help! I'm a Prisoner in the Library** Eth Clifford	$2.75
❏ MT44567-7	**Leah's Song** Eth Clifford	$2.75
❏ MT43618-X	**Me and Katie (The Pest)** Ann M. Martin	$2.75
❏ MT41529-8	**My Sister, The Creep** Candice F. Ransom	$2.75
❏ MT42883-7	**Sixth Grade Can Really Kill You** Barthe DeClements	$2.75
❏ MT40409-1	**Sixth Grade Secrets** Louis Sachar	$2.75
❏ MT42882-9	**Sixth Grade Sleepover** Eve Bunting	$2.75
❏ MT41732-0	**Too Many Murphys** Colleen O'Shaughnessy McKenna	$2.75

Available wherever you buy books, or use this order form.

- -

Scholastic Inc., P.O. Box 7502, 2931 East McCarty Street, Jefferson City, MO 65102

Please send me the books I have checked above. I am enclosing $_____ (please add $2.00 to cover shipping and handling). Send check or money order — no cash or C.O.D.s please.

Name _____

Address _____

City _____ **State/Zip** _____

Please allow four to six weeks for delivery. Offer good in the U.S.A. only. Sorry, mail orders are not available to residents of Canada. Prices subject to change.

APP591